The Morning after Darkness:

My Adoption Story

A Novel

Don Emerson

The Morning after Darkness:
My Adoption Journey

A Mckinney Publishing Production
Printing History: First Edition, January 2018
Library of Congress Control Number: 2018930148

ISBN: 978-1-943518-23-4

Characters, names, places, incidents, and situations are
the product of the author's imagination and invention,
or are used fictitiously. Any resemblance to actual
persons, living or dead, or events is coincidental.

Scripture quotations are from the ESV® Bible (The Holy Bible,
English Standard Version®), copyright © 2001 by Crossway, a
publishing ministry of Good News Publishers. Used by permission.
All rights reserved

For information address:
McKinney Publishing
www.McKinneyPublishing.com

This work was adapted from the original publication:
When the World Turns Upside Down: An Adoption Journey
Written by Donald (Don) G. Emerson
Published July 2016. ISBN 978-1-943518-13-5

Printed in the United States of America

Dedication

To my family: Sandy, Rod and Cindy, Dina and Randall, and my grandchildren Derek, Logan, Ellie, and Jack. And also, for our friends Glen Janzen, who enjoys Heaven, and his widow, Vicki.

"We seek serenity, and we acknowledge that we cannot find it unless we are willing to accept certain things because resisting unchangeable realities is not only unproductive but actually destructive.

--Father Jonathan Morris

Prologue

Sunday, October 5, 2008, Malibu, California

A small stretch of beach along the Pacific shoreline has always been a place I could quietly talk with God and find comfort. In my childhood many of my friends had found comfort talking to their dogs. Having no dog, I had found consolation walking along the sand, the Pacific waves rolling in, confiscating my troubles, washing them out to sea, restoring me. My parents had also found solace walking along this same stretch of Pacific sand.

There was something mysterious about looking out and seeing the azure sky meeting the blue-green ocean in the distance, much like that pot of gold at the end of the rainbow my parents told me about when I was a kid. As I'd look out at that point where sky met ocean, I knew from some distant place, far from shore, waves begin to build and move toward the sandy shoreline where I so often walked. During normal weather those waves always relaxed as they hit the sand and my bare feet, much like the peaceful effect this ambience had on me as I observed the nightfall from my insignificant spot above the ocean. The breeze off the Pacific was cool, but there was something about it reminiscent of my children's gentle touches when they were younger, warming, calming, loving, and comforting.

I'd spent my entire thirty-eight years of life in this house and on this property sitting above the ocean and this stretch of sand, a place I loved. As their refuge, my parents had purchased the property years before I was born. The house sat on four acres, surrounded by a security fence with alternating pink, white, and red oleander mostly obscuring it, the patio, and pool from the curious. Dad had always said the palm trees scattered about the grounds reminded him of San Jacinto, the small desert town about 60 miles east of Los Angeles, which he'd always called his hometown.

Why Dad called San Jacinto his hometown, having not spent a decade there as a kid, I never understood. Maybe it was simply because he'd been comfortable there. It was the place where he'd attended elementary school, and there he'd met Clifton Dunne and Ricardo Montgomery who were not only childhood friends but also two of his four closest, lifelong friends. Cliff and Rick had also been his business associates in adulthood -- Cliff, his accountant/business manager and Rick, his attorney; both now engaged by me in a similar capacity. Dad's other two closest friends were my mom and Billy Feldmann, the agent who had helped launch Dad's career. I'd known and respected all of them my entire life.

This house, which I loved, had always been a sort of mystery to me. Why was it so large? The two-storied, deep-red tile roofed, Spanish-styled stucco, was originally built in 1950 but enlarged and updated in the mid-1960s about the time Mom and Dad purchased it. The house, while spacious, certainly would be considered modest by current Malibu standards.

As I neared high school age, I always wondered why my parents had bought a house with five bedrooms, each with a bath, plus the master suite. After all, I was an only child. Had they intended filling the bedrooms with more children? Wondering about this was one thing, but asking either of them about it was something I'd never done.

The house and property had always been safe places for me growing up. Mom and Dad were a constant presence in my life. Dad's vocation afforded luxuries, including time. Mona, our long-standing cook and housekeeper, and her daughter Ginny, were my co-conspirators in adventures and mischief around the property and shore. Although I was never really lonely, I did have two ever-present feelings which relentlessly plagued me. The first was, "something is missing"; the second, even more disturbing, "I might be rejected." I never understood these troubling feelings until much later in life nor why I innately knew not to bring this up for discussion with Mom and Dad. My memories of growing up here, although filled with peaceful fondness, overlay that niggling agitation of something is "off." "Something is off" persisted and fermented, occasionally bubbling up from my subconscious demanding to have a voice.

After church this morning, Alle, the children, and I had spent much of the warm afternoon walking along the beach and swimming in the cool ocean, an echo from my childhood. I know now I belong here, but I hadn't felt I belonged sixteen years ago. Then, I'd felt like an interloper.

Our two children had gone to bed an hour earlier; school awaited them tomorrow. Alle was reading inside. I looked out at the ocean below, the setting sun striking the water creating a bright, reflective glow, as I sat on the deck off our bedroom observing the darkness descend and contemplating Pastor Sam's message this morning. Below on the lawn, the shadows danced to the music of the palms gently swaying in the breeze. I imagined I could faintly hear a lullaby such as Mom or Dad sang to me so long ago. Those melodious dancing palm shadows enhanced the calm and peacefulness I felt. The shadows that had followed me years ago weren't kind nor were they gentle. The descending darkness surrounding me now also seemed to reflect that time in my life when a different sort of darkness permeated my life. Darkness and shadows were my nemeses then, the time in my life when my world capsized.

"Life isn't always a neat bundle of happiness. Each of us encounter face-to-face challenges--pain, grief, adversity, or whatever word one uses to label. Will the challenges we face today be those we face tomorrow? Perhaps so, but that may well depend upon our response to those challenges. My own life experience indicates that even more important than the challenges we face is our response to them." Pastor Sam's sermon comments had struck me at the moment of utterance, a clap of thunder or bolt of lightning. I quickly realized why as I sat in the pew. My life had cracked 16 years before.

As my world capsized, the darkness and shadows I faced then certainly seemed they might forever be my tomorrows. The remaining part of the only family I'd ever known had been snatched from me. My father's last words to me had been "Christine" and "adopted." I learned the word "adopted" applied to me.

Discovering I had been adopted was almost indescribable. My breathing had stopped as my soul peeled away from my body. I stood immobile and watched my body cling to an elevator of all that was familiar as the cables dangled useless to stop my plunging into an unknown abyss. Everything I had known, the framework of my life, had shattered. I wondered how to fill the aching void? Alone I had never been, but alone I felt. My heart ached for the presence and comfort of my Dad or Mom. They simply could not be replaced, nor their presence and comfort filled by any other. I had the double ache of wondering who I really was after having spent over two decades thinking I knew and how I could rebuild an image of who I was. This shocking revelation would only be processed with time. I recall breathing again, the first step in my process of transformation and acceptance. Time was my ally and worked wonders, plus a few lucky events. Did I say, *lucky events*? Perhaps they were not luck at all.

Christine, whom I had located 16 years ago per Dad's last request, and Ben, her husband and lawyer, had recently asked my permission to use Dad's journals, Mom's diaries, and my own life for a film project she'd been considering. I hadn't known either Christine or Ben until I was in my early twenties, but we were now close. We were family. I had agreed to their request, somewhat reluctantly. The truth is, the story was about as much their story as mine anyway, but I'd appreciated their asking my permission. Each of our life trajectories had strangely crossed sixteen years ago. With the assistance I now provided them, our stories would soon become public. Did I want or need my life, our lives, projected on a big screen for the world to see? No, I didn't. Our privacy had been an area which Dad and Mom had carefully safeguarded over the years, and now as an adult, privacy also felt safe to me. I realized my desire for closure and my life experiences were less important than the potential life-changing benefit for someone else. That beneficial aspect had been upper-most in my thinking when I'd agreed to assist on the project.

Chapter One

Saturday June 6, 1992, Malibu, Afternoon,

Immediately after my graduation from the University of Arizona, I had flown home. Memories became my seat companions on the flight from Tucson to Los Angeles; I totally ignored those seated around me. I wasn't trying to be rude; I knew I needed those memories on this trip, probably the last time I'd spend moments with my dad.

As soon as I had stored my carry-on in the over-head bin and taken my seat, a little boy about eight or nine with a bandage around the top of his head and his mother took the two seats in front of me. Seeing that little guy brought back memories of Mom and Dad telling me once about a head injury I'd suffered when I was young as a result of darting out in front of a car.

Mom and Dad always said my recovery had been their second miracle. After being hit by the car, I'd been in a coma-like state for about eight hours prior to regaining consciousness, at which time my mind backed up to just prior to my darting out into the street. I seemed normal mentally, but over the next few days in the hospital I had problems moving my left leg and foot normally. On the tenth day, when I was released from the hospital, all physical problems had disappeared. Two weeks following the accident, I was examined by my pediatrician. Following his examination, which Mom said consisted of a number of mental tests and physical activities, the pediatrician had looked at Mom and Dad and said, "There should still be some lingering problems as a result of the head injury Lance suffered, but I find none. Someone upstairs looked after him for you." Mom and Dad always remained thankful to that "someone upstairs."

For some reason I never understood, Mom and Dad shared few stories about their life prior to my coming along, but two of the stories they did share always seemed to amuse them and me.

First, Mom was never much of a cook. Both of my parents were fond of telling the story of her making Dad's favorite dessert, coconut pie, while they were dating. After Dad ate a piece, she asked how it was. His facial expression and reply, "This is great. Just like Mom's. You must have a taste," had communicated two different messages. Mom grabbed a fork and swallowed a piece of her pie. The pie was dreadful. After going into the kitchen to put her fork in the sink, she noticed the sugar she'd forgotten to add still sitting on the kitchen counter. Both of them always laughed telling the story. The garbage consumed the rest of the pie, and Dad took Mom out to dinner. Soon after they married and Dad's salary increased, they hired a cook and housekeeper, Mona Washington.

Second, Dad's discovery had been a bit quirky. After seeing Mom's and Dad's performances in a production of Who's Afraid of Virginia Woolf?, Billy Feldmann told Dad over coffee the next morning he had a role perfect for him, the lead in a WWII drama, From the Brink of Hell. The role was a captured GI, imprisoned by the Germans and presumed dead, only to return from the war to discover his wife involved in a new relationship. Dad's reply to Billy's offer had been, "Yes, I'm interested, but I need to make something clear to you. I'm a Christian." Billy's response had been, "Devin, I've found you an interesting young man with an interesting shy-like charisma. You're a first. No one has ever told me before they were a Christian when I asked if they had interest in a screen test. That I like. Being Jewish sometimes creates problems for me. I admire you and will always be supportive. Your guy-next-door appeal will jump off the screen." A few weeks later Dad had a successful screen test and accepted the contract offer. Dad and Billy's future business and personal relationship seemed anchored in those first comments.

Lost in memories, I must, at some point, have drifted off to sleep, only to awaken when a rather bumpy descent jolted me back to the present sorrowful reality.

Mona had driven out to LAX in Dad's car to "fetch me." "Fetch" was a term commonly used in Mom's family for some reason. I recall Dad once telling Mom her use of the term was incorrect; and the term should only be used in relation to things. Mom's quick retort, "I don't care, Dev. The phrase was good enough for my grandmother, so it's good enough for me, thank you," halted any further response from Dad.

Mona and her daughter, Ginny, had always been favorites of mine. Not only had I always had two wonderful parents who loved me, Mona and Ginny did too.

Unlike previous flights home Mona had never been sent to "fetch me," but Dad could no longer perform that duty.

Mona and I always had a warm and loving relationship and could converse for hours. However, this trip from LAX to the house was not one spent in easy conversation. Shortly after we left the airport I asked how Dad was doing. Mona only said, "Not good and declining quickly." Noticing she was on the verge of tears, I shifted the conversation to my graduation hours before. She seemed amused we'd roasted under the blazing Tucson sun, sitting on folding chairs awaiting our turn to cross the portable stage to receive a piece of parchment. The only place on campus large enough to accommodate the number of graduates and the large crowd of well-wishers was the football stadium.

Mona was curious as to why the graduation hadn't been held in the evening when it was cooler. That was an interesting thought as graduation under the blazing sun had been sweat-drenchingly uncomfortable.

As soon as we'd arrived at the house, the dark reality struck me, a painful tsunami, washing away any lingering happy memories.

Entering the house, I had gone immediately to Dad's room. The room had changed. Mom and Dad's bed had been moved against a wall, its original spot in the room now occupied by a hospital bed on which I saw my sleeping Dad. He was dreadfully pale and looked as though he'd lost over half his weight since he'd visited me weeks earlier in Tucson. Much about the room seemed the same, except for medical paraphernalia on a nightstand and on the table which always rested between Mom's and Dad's recliners. Dad's sister, my Aunt Alexa, was sleeping in one of the two recliners, now moved close to Dad's hospital bed. Also in the room, I noticed a nurse returning a blood pressure monitor to the table. Seeing me enter, she motioned for me to be quiet and follow her into the hall.

As soon as she had quietly closed the bedroom door, she said, "You must be Lance."

"I am. How's Dad?"

"He's hanging on. He's not awake much, but he was anxious for you to come home when he was awake more often. I'm Alice, the head nurse on your father's case."

"Glad to meet you, even under these circumstances. I should have left the university and come home before graduation, but Dad insisted I stay there."

"I know. Your Aunt Alexa told me."

"When will they wake, Alice?"

"When Devin's awake now it's not for long; his pain meds contribute to so much sleep. Your aunt usually doesn't nap during the day but was awake a lot last evening. She asked me to tell you to go to your dad's study if you arrived while she was asleep. Your father left some things on his desk for you."

"Thanks. That's where I'll be then should she wake up."

I walked downstairs and into the study. I'd always been comfortable in Dad's study. The dark walnut paneling and bookcases might have made the room much too dark had it not been for the two large windows along one wall allowing bright sunlight to enter the room. The many family pictures, plus a few photos of Mom and Dad attending premieres, also tended to add brightness. Some said Dad's large rosewood desk seemed a bit out of place. Its color, they said, clashed with the dark walnut in the room. Dad liked the desk which he'd purchased years ago at some estate sale in Beverly Hills, a desk having once belonged to some silent screen star. Dad always responded to criticism about his desk by saying, "Who cares whether the desk's color clashes with the walls? I certainly don't. It's just a desk. I like it."

Growing up, I had spent lots of time in this room sitting on the sofa or in one of the two arm chairs doing homework while Dad worked at his desk or learned lines for his next day's shoot, and Mom read, both willing to help when I needed assistance. It had also been the room in which Mom and I had a number of more or less friendly confrontations regarding my wanting to play contact sports at school and her saying that would be too dangerous because of the head injury I'd suffered. But the most vivid and interesting memory of all those I had of Dad's study was that obligatory father-son conversation we'd had regarding the "birds and bees" shortly before I entered ninth grade. Don't all boys recall such a conversation? I've never forgotten that conversation. After I told him I'd already heard from friends most of what he'd said, I clearly recall his last words before telling me I could leave, "Remember Lance, there's a time and place for everything. Not everything which is right feels good, and not everything which feels good is right. You can never go wrong if you keep your pants up and zipped." How like Dad to use those words. The memory always brought a smile. As simplistic and humorous as Dad's comments may have been, I had known there was truth in them.

Sitting at his desk I noticed the four black-bound books stacked on the left and three multi-colored ones on the right.

Those must be what Dad had left for me. Glancing briefly through the top ones on each stack, I was surprised to discover they were Dad's journals and Mom's diaries. I'd never known or seen either of them do such writing.

I returned Mom's first diary to the stack, picked up the journal on top, and began reading Dad's first entry.

Friday, December 19, 1958

We'd met in September in an English class shortly after I arrived on the University of Arizona campus to begin my sophomore year. This evening had been our one and only Christmas gift exchange. Things weren't supposed to have turned out this way. That night weeks ago shouldn't have happened. The night still haunts. I explained all this tonight and how I felt to Anna, but I'm not certain she even wanted to understand. We'll see.

When I'd opened the package and saw her gift, this blank book, I must have had a perplexed expression because Anna looked at me, laughed, and said, "Devin, it's a journal. You write things in it. You need to begin doing that. When you're famous, and you will be, how can you possibly write your autobiography or someone write a biography of your life? You must have some record."

I'd said nothing for seconds. A bit confused, I just looked at this leather-bound, lined volume I held in my hands.

When I looked up, Anna was smiling sadly, no doubt recalling my earlier words about ending our relationship, and said, "Believe me, Devin, you'll come to enjoy the journal. It'll become your friend, your new friend. It will also be great therapy."

"Anna, only someone majoring in psychology would say that. That's not your major."

"I know, Devin, but just write in it for a few weeks. You'll see."

"Okay, I will, but I'm skeptical."

"Writing in it will clear your head, and the journal will become your friend. Trust me."

"If you say so, Anna, I'll believe it for now."

Book, or whatever I should call you, maybe we will become friends over the next few months. We'll see, won't we?

I'd never heard either Dad or Mom mention an Anna before. I wondered who she was. An old girlfriend? What did the sentence really mean, "That night weeks ago shouldn't have happened"? Only one thing came to mind, but contemplating that was difficult. I remember my Dad as always being in control. Dad was perfect. Was I blind, naïve, or what? Have I been so sheltered, I have difficulty accepting reality? Have I lived with this man all my life and never really known him? I had no definitive answers.

I closed my eyes as if that might make the uncomfortable thoughts go away. They didn't, of course, so I returned to reading the journal.

Monday, January 5, 1959

What am I really supposed to call you? Or do I call you anything? I need a name, I think. For lack of another term, I'll just call you, Journal.

So Journal, a new year has begun, and here I am for our first real session.

My two weeks of Christmas break at home with Mom, Dad, and Alex proved relaxing and enjoyable. A nice break from the university and thoughts of Anna, but Oklahoma isn't Arizona. I much prefer Tucson, its sun and warmth, especially in December.

Even though I've ended our relationship, I still think about Anna and what happened, but those thoughts are no longer coming as often, and I have less guilt.

Anna! The relationship had to end. Otherwise, I'd have had guilt feelings each time I was with her.

Visiting with Mom and Alex over Christmas break refreshed me as always, but Dad... What can I say? He never changes, and neither does our relationship.

Journal, I suppose I need to tell you a bit about myself. We can't become real friends without my sharing, can we? I know your background; it's rather blank, isn't it? So, as briefly as possible, I'll tell you mine.

I was born on July 16, 1938, in a small town in southern Oklahoma, my father's hometown, a town so small it had to be your destination to even get there. And then, if you managed to get there and sneezed, you were blown past. It was the town where my parents met after my maternal grandmother divorced, and Mom and grandmother left that windblown, dusty farm outside Plainview, Texas, and moved to my great grandparent's equally dusty, run-down Oklahoma farm. The farm and town were tired and rusty, not just the result of the depression and drought but more because of isolation and the inhabitants' limited exposure to an outside world. Living not too far apart, my parents eventually met and married. Alex and I were their bonus. Well, I'm sure there were times they didn't consider us much of a bonus but more like the lingering throb resulting from missing the nail but finding your thumb.

Four years later, Dad moved us to San Jacinto, California. Mom was delighted. Civilization finally!

World War II was raging. Dad, who had always loved to tinker with automobiles, joined the military and had been assigned to Ryan Air Attack Base in the Hemet area as an airplane mechanic.

My legal name is Devin MacArthur Bradshaw, but I hope to be better known as Devin MacArthur when I become a professional.

"Why was I named Devin MacArthur?" I once asked Mom. Her annoyed look sent some unknown message, yet she responded, "You were named after an old boyfriend." That was all I was ever told. A closed book it became, never to open again. I had no clue whether it was true, but I always found the idea mysterious and appealing, a statement in which I must have taken some pride. Otherwise, why has her response remained etched in my mind?

My sister, Alexa Kaitlyn Bradshaw, a tall redhead, whom I've always called Alex, was named for mom's brother, our Uncle Alexander. Of that, I'm certain. It wasn't a family secret. In my case, maybe there really was a boyfriend. Strange to think your mother had a boyfriend, someone other than your father.

As a kid, I found California exciting. I grew to love the aroma permeating the San Jacinto Valley, a unique blend of freshly plowed and fertilized fields and orange and lemon blossoms. During the years after my family left California, I always missed the aroma of those fields and blossoms and longed to return. But while we lived there, the frequent visits to my maternal grandmother's apartment in downtown Los Angeles, where she had moved after Uncle Alexander joined the Navy, were the ultimate in excitement. I could punch those buttons and ride that elevator up and down, especially when the elevator operator wasn't on duty. My own toy! There were also frequent drives to the ocean and into the mountains, trips to Long Beach and the Boardwalk with that huge roller coaster going out over the ocean, and the weekend trips to the Navy piers in San Diego to meet Uncle Alexander when his ship was in port.

Staying inside, behind blackout curtains, with the piercing air raid sirens blaring was one of three frightening experiences I recall from my childhood. The sound of blaring sirens and the danger they signaled remain ingrained. I still experience dread on hearing sirens. This was different, however, from the fear of my second frightening memory - getting lost at the Boardwalk in Long Beach. I'd been told to stand beside by grandmother while Mom and Dad went through the Fun House, some sort of glass and mirrored maze. Somehow, grandmother and I got separated for a few minutes. Talk about panic! I did. I still sometimes fear being left. The third frightening thing from those days was my first encounter with a snake. Thinking it was a stick, I picked up a snake as it was sunning in the grass. When it moved, I threw it as fast as I could. That was the origin of my fear of snakes; a fear which remains to this day.

I began kindergarten at San Jacinto Elementary where I would remain a student for a number of years, a place where my natural curiosity expanded. It was there also that I met my two best friends, Cliff and Rick. Since those elementary years, our threesome has remained in periodic contact. I'm sure we'll renew our close friendship once we're each involved in our chosen professions, and I return to California.

A few years following the end of the war, Dad moved us back to Oklahoma. Dad took over my grandfather's automobile dealership. It was located in a city miles away from my birthplace and more engaged in the world. Dad's dealership was affiliated with the Ford Motor Company, which is the root of my propensity to drive Ford cars.

Early on, I developed an intense interest in motion pictures, fostered by my parents often taking Alex and me to the movies. To Mom and Dad, movies were a family event, not a parental activity where children were shuffled off to sitters. The one movie of the era I've always recalled is <u>To Each His Own</u>, starring Olivia De Havilland and John Lund, the story of an unwed mother who gives up her son and remains separated from him for 25 years. The movie left a deep impression. It was so deeply sad. I don't understand why the movie had such an impact. Maybe someday, I will.

During the balance of my school years after leaving San Jacinto, throughout high school and the university, I never had friendships to compare with Cliff and Rick. My new passions were movies and music. I was odd-man out, having little interest in sports. I excelled in track only. Consequently, I was not one of the popular kids in school. Someone once asked me why I was such a fast runner. My reply, "Must be the yellow streak running down my back," was met only with a blank stare. My humor arrow missed its mark.

Dad spent long hours working and most of his down-time in front of the television. When my school acquaintances talked about hunting and fishing with their fathers, I longed to have that experience. Dad was always too busy. In high school, long after I developed other interests, Dad approached me about going fishing and hunting. I always declined. I was never sure if I declined because I no longer had any interest, or because declining would pay back Dad for ignoring me earlier.

I did, however, have a close relationship with my mother. Mom shared my interests and rejoiced in my achievements, just as she did in Alexa's. Mom always said her grandfather was a Cherokee Indian, whether she looked like one or not. She also had family members who were of different religious persuasions. With them she freely discussed religious beliefs. She found the beliefs they shared in common, and discarded those on which they disagreed as unimportant or trivial. Thus, Alexa and I grew to have a bit more tolerance than did most of our school peers.

In high school, theatre entered my life. It became my life blood and has remained a passion, alongside my interest in movies and music. I enjoyed the thrill of performing before an audience. Crawling into another's skin allowed an escape from my reserved nature. Being another character became an addiction--an experience akin to what some people must feel with drugs or alcohol. Performing became my addiction of choice, albeit a safe one.

Upon graduation from high school, I rejected a scholarship to the University of Oklahoma in favor of a small college in eastern Oklahoma with an acclaimed theatre teacher. Dr. Frank was a tough task-master. She demanded the best. You gave it to her or else. There a different kind of passion entered my life, a young lady. The relationship fell apart by the end of my freshman year. The ending of the relationship, plus a desire to go west again, led me to enroll as a sophomore at the University of Arizona in Tucson. There I earned my BA in theatre and stayed to complete my master's degree.

Well, Journal, that's about it for tonight. Our first session! I feel great. Maybe Anna was right. My conversations with you may well turn out to be therapeutic. We'll see. Off to bed now.

Neither Mom nor Dad had shared much information with me about life before they came to California and Dad began his career. I'd always wanted to know more. When Dad did share, the information wasn't delivered in any depth. Most of this information was new to me. So Anna was definitely a girlfriend, but the sort of relationship Dad wrote about here seemed so unlike my Dad. Dad's relationship with my grandfather was also foreign to me, but I'd never seen my grandparents much for some reason. All this was so strange. Dad and I always had a very close relationship, unlike what Dad had written about his own relationship with my grandfather. That made me uncomfortable. How had it influenced Dad?

I suddenly remembered Dad lying upstairs gravely ill. How strange to even contemplate his impending death. I'd never given much thought in my younger years to a parent dying. I suppose that's normal.

Death is one of life's great mysteries. With my Christian views on death, why was it a mystery? Death doesn't blow a trumpet. It creeps or blasts in. All enter its door. Eventually! It had touched me once before. I should have known it could touch me again, but it touching me again had never entered my consciousness for some reason. I knew Dad's death was coming, had known for weeks since his visit to Tucson, but knowing hadn't made the approaching moment any easier.

I closed and replaced the journal on the stack, rose, and left the room to find Alice. I found her sitting in a chair outside Dad's bedroom reading a book.

"Are they both still asleep, Alice?"

"Yes, they are. I just looked in the room a few minutes ago."

"Then, if either wakes, let them know I'm going to visit Mom and will be back soon."

"Okay, Lance, I'll do that." I couldn't help but notice the puzzled look on her face, but chose not to explain "visiting my Mom" further.

It had been my ritual for four years each time I'd come home. Why should it be different this time, even if Dad was deathly ill? Besides, he was asleep. Even if awake, perhaps he wouldn't be coherent. I had to visit Mom, needed those visits with her.

I stopped at a flower shop on the way where I'd always bought her roses. Red roses. Her favorite. She'd always had a rose garden around the patio. As a kid, I enjoyed helping her tend it. While I probably wasn't much help, she always welcomed me there, another of her ways of making me feel loved and important.

Parking the car sometime later, I took the roses off the seat, and walked down the path lined with trees. The lush green, carefully-manicured, rolling lawn dotted with trees created a beautiful vista. Arriving where Mom now rested, I placed the roses in the copper vases on each side of her headstone. Then I sat on the grass, and soon thoughts of her flooded me.

She'd left us four years ago. Four years! That's an eternity when you miss someone. And how I missed her! I wanted her to hold me to ease my current pain as she did when I was a kid. The future's going to be difficult. Mom wouldn't share it. What does that say about me, a grown man needing his mother? I'm sure it says I love and need her. Still. Aunt Alexa is here, but she's not Mom, and I really don't know her well. It won't be the same. Dad could no longer hold me, but I guess I'll be holding him. I still wondered about Mom's accident. She'd asked me to go with her. I should have, but I wanted to visit with high school friends. That day loops through my mind, much like one of Dad's films. I couldn't have had a better mother. She was the greatest.

Knowing I had to get back to the house, I rose as my eyes fell once again upon those words which always stirred me prior to leaving this beautiful and serene resting place.

Erin Evans Bradshaw
Born - February 14, 1941
Died - July 7, 1988
Beloved wife of Dev and mother of Lance
And now these remain: Faith, Hope, and
Love
But the greatest of these is Love.

Looking at those words on the headstone, I said once again as I always did just before leaving, "Mom, I love and miss you."

I turned and walked slowly back to the car, resisting the urge to look back, unlike I had done four years ago.

Then, at the conclusion of Mom's graveside service, Dad and I had just remained seated looking at her casket. Pastor Sam had finally come up behind us, placed a hand on each of our shoulders and said, "Devin, Lance, I'll walk with you to the limo now. As if in some trance, we both rose and moved toward the vehicle, Sam between us, an arm around each of our waists, but I remember looking back. Why? I don't recall, but it had been so hard to leave her then. Leaving this time was not as hard.

Chapter Two

Driving back to the house from the cemetery, my visit with Dad in Tucson a few weeks earlier kept playing in my head. He had seemed his old self then, unlike the father asleep upstairs when I'd left the house to visit Mom's grave. At least he seemed his old self physically.

Dad had flown to Tucson to tell me the end was near. He hadn't wasted away at that point. His appearance that day coming off the plane was much like the father I had always known, but his travelling attire was unusual for him.

Dad's blue-green eyes missed nothing. He'd always been a big man. His 6'3" height and 179 pound, muscularly-slender build were enhanced by broad shoulders. His size didn't often allow him an occasion to remain unnoticed, yet he preferred to go unnoticed, unlike many public figures. I always found that ironic for someone in the public eye. Dad was never unnoticed when in public, often to his distress.

His sun-bleached, streaked, sandy-blond hair was always slightly wavy, longish at the nape of his neck and touching the top of or slightly over his ears. There had been noticeable gray the last six or seven years, but he had no interest in hiding that. More mature roles came his way. Mom had liked the gray forming at his temples. "Distinguished," she had said. However, the gray had become much more pronounced, especially after he lost his hair to chemo, and it had grown back. His hair almost always had that wind-blown appearance. Even coming off the plane his hair appeared to have met with a bit of wind.

Those who didn't know him well usually thought he was just another of those handsome dudes who reveled or gloated in his good looks. However, those who knew him best were well aware that Dad took little pride in his looks, but his dress was another matter. He'd always said his looks were not his doing. He believed one should take pride in one's accomplishments and behavior, just not too much. Arrogance was foreign to him.

I always thought Dad was a stylish dresser. His profession demanded he be well-dressed, but I'm confident he'd always wanted to dress well regardless of his profession. He tended to wear jeans or shorts, a polo shirt, and tennis shoes around our house, but when out in public, he usually preferred to wear slacks, short or long-sleeved shirts, maybe a sports coat, and his loafers. He only wore dress shoes when he was required to wear a suit and tie or a tuxedo. But he much preferred to avoid those occasions altogether. He and Mom had that in common.

How I'd miss Dad's "look." I was always pleased that many thought I looked a lot like him. I'd sometimes tried to imitate "his look," but not too successfully or as frequently as he'd have preferred. My imitation didn't seem to please Dad at first, but Mom always told him, "Dev, leave him alone. He's not in the public eye, and he dresses well, I think. He needs to make his own decisions." Dad seldom said much after that; he always deferred to Mom when there was a disagreement. I found this unusual but interesting.

As Dad had entered the airport gate waiting area in Tucson that morning I noted he was wearing shorts, a polo shirt, and loafers without socks, not normal travelling attire for him. He had perched his sunglasses atop his head. He'd immediately spotted me, standing in back of the waiting crowd as I held hands with my beautiful and blonde girlfriend. I'd told Dad about her a few times on the phone. I opened my arms and hugged him tightly, "Great to see you, Dad. You look a little tired."

"I'm okay, Lance," he whispered as we embraced.

I turned toward my friend and said, "Dad, this is the girlfriend I've told you about, Shelby Alaina Morgan. She prefers

Alle." She was a natural blonde like Mom and preferred casual dress also. Her blue eyes were piercing, never looking away in conversation which always made me feel her interest never wavered. Alle was one of those girls who refused to join a sorority. A bit too "uppity" for her.

"I'm delighted to meet you, Alle. Please call me, Devin."

"I'm glad to finally meet you. Lance has told me so much about you." Alle would never have called an older person by a first name at the first meeting.

"Hope it was all good."

"Oh, it was. Lance has great admiration for you."

I took Dad's carry-on as we moved out of the building toward the parking area.

Once out of the airport and headed to my little house just east of campus, the discussion turned to Alle, native of Scottsdale where her father was an Arizona State University math professor and her mother a high school English teacher. Naturally, Alle wanted to teach—high school English. It made sense that she would interest me; I was seriously considering a teaching career also rather than following in Dad's career tracks. Billy, Dad's agent, was always nagging me to pursue film, but neither Dad nor Mom pushed me in either direction. Dad seemed to be taken with Alle. I was pleased.

Arriving at the house, Alle said her goodbyes and headed for Scottsdale to visit her family.

As Dad and I settled down in the living room, I said, "Okay Dad, what's going on? Something's wrong, isn't it? You're not okay, are you?"

"I'm just fine. Bought the <u>Los Angeles Times</u> and read it on the flight over. I wasn't listed on the obituary pages, so I'm doing okay."

"Dad, I know you like to say that, but I don't see much humor in it at the moment." I knew something was amiss.

"I understand."

"So tell me. What's wrong?"

"Lance, there's no easy way to do this; the lung cancer is back. I found out a few days ago. It has spread and is now inoperable. Nothing more can be done."

"What? And you didn't call me? Get a second opinion!"

"That's not needed. The oncologist said there's no effective treatment currently available. I know she's correct."

"You can't even have chemo again or radiation?"

"I could, but there's only a five percent chance of success."

"Dad, five percent is better than no chance."

"That may be, but you remember how sick I was before?"

"Well, you're still here, aren't you?"

"Yeah, but the cancer's back."

"Then do something about it."

"Lance, I'm not putting myself through that treatment again."

"You have to, for me and for yourself." How could he even consider no treatment?

"No, I'm not going through that again just to gain a few months."

"Why not?" I paused. "What's the best prognosis then?" I could feel the tears welling. That old feeling of rejection or abandonment briefly hit me. Why now?

"I have weeks, but no more than four months probably. I feel basically okay now though."

"Weeks?"

"At least we have some time. Neither of us had that with your mother."

"And that's supposed to make this easier for me?"

"Well, no, but…"

"No buts. This isn't easy. Can't you understand that?" How could my dad just seem to give up? "Dad, I've lost Mom. I'm now supposed to lose you too?" The tears began to escape and roll down my cheeks.

Dad moved over to the couch, put his arm around my shoulder, and I was transported back to being a kid again being consoled by Dad. I sobbed uncontrollably, aware of a familiar, yet incongruent feeling of being cherished and abandoned gnawing at my consciousness.

"I know this is difficult for you. But we have to face it. Life isn't always fair. It doesn't come with guarantees. When handed a death sentence, we make the best of a bad thing. I've had more time to think about this and get some distance. You have not had that time to process any of this yet."

"There's not a 'best' in this bad thing, Dad." I moved out of his embrace and looked at him. "Can't you see that?" I was being uncharacteristically defiant. This was so unlike me. The compliant child was balking at a confrontation threatening to rip my reality into shreds. The ever-present gnawing of "something is missing" and "I'm being rejected" clashed wildly inside. I had few tools to deal with this catastrophic upheaval. I allowed my dad's words to seep into my brain. Gradually, I began to breathe again. The terror and confusion scaled down a few notches.

"Lance, we have to do the best we can. Maybe a miracle will come along."

"Do the best we can? A miracle will come along? Those words are not too comforting and certainly not reassuring. I'll come home."

"You can't. There's only a few weeks before you graduate."

"Dad, I have to. I need time with you. I can still graduate."

"What I want is for you to stay here. Seeing you graduate from our alma mater was our dream, your mother's and mine."

"I should come home and spend time with you."

"Please don't come home until after your graduation. We'll have time after you graduate."

"I should come on home."

"Don't come home until after your graduation."

"I can make arrangements with my professors. I don't have to be physically present at this point in order to graduate."

"As I said earlier, I want you to stay here. We can talk on the phone every day. Your Aunt Alex will be coming to stay with me. She and I will plan the details when she flies out on Monday. She'll keep you informed."

"I'd rather be at home with you, Dad."

"Ah, son, I appreciate that. Regardless of how many people are around, there are some things we all do alone. Martin Luther once said something to the effect that every man must do two things alone; he must do his own believing and his own dying."

"That may be true, Dad, but I think there might be some comfort having me around." My emotions and thinking began to be responsive to his words and choices.

"I won't be alone. Until you graduate and are home, Alex will be with me."

"I don't like this, but... You better still be around the after-noon following my graduation because after I walk that stage, I'm catching the first plane home."

"I promise. Now, I'd like some lunch."

"Where?"

"Let's go to the Student Union. I'm still strong enough to walk there from here."

*****

As we sat at our table a bit later, I said, "Okay, Dad, what'll you have? I'll get it."

"A grilled cheese and a chocolate shake."

"I'll be right back."

After we had eaten, I noticed him looking toward an area near one of the exit doors. "Dad, what do you see?"

"Lance, it was at a table over there where I first saw your moth-er sitting with a guy named Chuck, her high school friend."

"Is that when you met her?"

"Oh, no, that happened about an hour later when she was in the first class I attended my last year here. So, how did you meet Alle?"

"She took a theatre elective, and I saved her life."

"You didn't?"

"Well, not really, but I continue to tell her I did."

"Tell me about it."

"We were in theatre lighting together. A three-hour lab on Tuesdays was a requirement."

"I remember those labs. Not much has changed."

"Well, one afternoon we were hanging lights for a show. Some freshman was on the pin rail adding weights to the weight carriage. The brake slipped, or he hadn't secured it properly, and up flew the light batten to the grid. Someone yelled, "Everyone, offstage!" Alle was standing next to me. I grabbed her around the waist and carried her offstage."

"Anyone hurt?"

"No. One of the cables broke, the batten came loose when it hit the grid, a lighting instrument came crashing to the stage floor, and counter weights came crashing down from the pin rail. Someone would have been killed if one of those weights or lights from that height had hit them. We had a bent pipe batten, damaged lights, but no injuries."

"You guys were lucky. So maybe you did save her life?"

"I keep reminding her of that. And we've been an item since."

"She's a lovely young lady."

"Oh, she is. And her parents are great also."

"So this is really serious?"

"It is now." I paused briefly as I tried to assess his expression. "Does that bother you?"

"Not at all. She reminds me of your mother. You'd be lucky to marry someone like your mom."

"Believe me, I've thought about that. I'm a lucky guy." I was so glad Dad had no objections to my being in a serious relationship. "Now what do you want to do next?"

"Our last stop. I want to go up Mount Lemmon and sit at a picnic table."

"Why?"

"Every Sunday in the summer after we'd attended church, except when we went to your grandparents' in Scottsdale, your mom and I would pack a picnic lunch, get the Sunday <u>Los Angeles Times</u>, drive to the top of Mount Lemmon, park near a picnic table, have lunch, and read the newspaper. It was about twenty degrees cooler up there than down here in Tucson, and cool was welcomed during those hot months."

"It's beautiful up there. I always thought it odd you could be on top of a mountain about an hour or so from Tucson. Ever ski up there?"

"No, never drove up there when the ski area was open. We just went for the cooler temps in the summer, not to become ice cubes in the winter."

*****

An hour or so later we were among the tall pines and sitting at a picnic table.

"Okay, Dad, what's so special about being up here?"

"Mostly, remembering the wonderful times I spent here with your mother."

"What did you talk about?"

"We didn't have to talk. Just being with her was enough. Ever feel that with your Alle?"

"I often do. In fact, being with her doesn't require conversation."

"Then you have something special with that girl. Don't lose it."

"I know I do, and I definitely won't lose it."

"You know, it was up here that I proposed to your mother."

He shared the story. It was a story I found hard to believe and seemed strange behavior for the Dad I knew. Mom, no doubt, was fascinated by him. Dad must have been obsessed with her.

"Lance, I want you to use her wedding ring when that time comes for you. It carries a special magic."

"I will. Thanks, Dad. I enjoyed the drive and appreciate all you've shared with me. That means a lot, especially now."

When we returned to my house, Dad said, "Thanks for allowing me to have all these moments with you. I've enjoyed it."

"I did too, Dad."

"If you don't mind, I'd like to go to bed now. I'm exhausted."

"Are you okay?"

"I'm fine, just really tired. I'll be fine in the morning."

We both slept in until 9 a.m. the next morning. After dressing, I scrambled eggs for us. Then it was time to get to the airport for Dad's flight back to LAX.

Just before Dad boarded the plane back to LAX, we embraced, and I whispered in his ear, "You and Mom were the best. Remember your promise to be there after my graduation. I love you."

"I love you too. Always remember that. Who knows? Maybe it's miracle time."

I don't think either Dad or I really believed there would be a miracle.

Dad turned and slowly passed through his boarding gate without looking back. I recall thinking, *I hope he's still okay after I graduate. I need more time with him.*

That wasn't to be though. He's confined to his bed and uncommunicative. I want to talk with him again.

Chapter Three

Devin's Journal, Friday, April 10, 1992

I'd arrived a bit early in the office complex parking garage this morning. On the drive in there had been bright sun, a cool ocean breeze, what should have been a beautiful day. It wasn't to be.

I'd felt apprehensive as I entered the office, registered, and sat down. The overused magazines failed to hold my interest. Good Housekeeping, Redbook, Sports Illustrated, and Gentlemen's Quarterly just didn't do it. I simply couldn't concentrate. Those tests had probed and prodded my entire body. I'd wondered if all those x-rays and scans had left me with an overdose of radiation. All that radiation could kill someone. My mind wandered. I couldn't relax, sweat formed on my forehead. Anticipation panic might have overwhelmed me, but the nurse called my name.

I rose and followed her, thinking maybe I'd bill the doctor for the time I'd waited. I chuckled at the thought of seeing the doctor's face after reading the invoice. At least, the thought was a humorous diversion.

She directed me down a hallway, through a doorway, and into a room. "Please wait in here. The doctor will be with you shortly," she said. I sat in one of the two chairs facing the desk.

It was a professional's office, not the typical patient room, carpeted, with an executive desk, credenza holding what appeared to be family photos, and medical degrees hanging on two walls. The room created a calming, relaxing atmosphere, provided one could relax. Intentional obviously.

I recalled what Dr. Wray had told me about this specialist. I was her favorite actor, and she didn't look forward to seeing me for two reasons: 1) she thought I was a nice person based on all she'd read, so giving me any bad news would be difficult for her, and 2) she had sat in an office with her father years before while a doctor had given them bad news about her terminally ill mother. Her desire to become a doctor had been emotionally and mentally imbedded that moment.

I just hoped Dr. Williams had some good news regarding treatment options for me.

Momentarily, a dowdy, graying brunette entered, smiled rather sadly, and sat behind the desk. She looked at me briefly as though I was familiar. I suppose I was familiar, but to my knowledge she'd never seen me without makeup.

She opened my folder, reviewed the contents, looked at me over her glasses, and said, "I'm Dr. Williams. Dr. Wray requested I see you about possible treatment options. She forwarded all your records and tests. Do you prefer I call you Mr. MacArthur or Mr. Bradshaw?"

"Either would be fine, Doctor, but if you don't mind, I'd prefer you call me Devin." I uncrossed my legs and sat upright.

"Devin, it will be then. I've carefully reviewed all your records, tests, everything." I flinched. Did her voice carry a hint of the ominous? My gut tightened and I felt perspiration on my forehead. She had paused, looking at the folder contents again.

I thought, oh great. Here comes the wrecking ball.

A wrecking ball it had been. No good news, no treatment options available, just a short time left.

The remainder of the meeting remains a bit of a blur, but I recall Dr. Williams saying, "Devin, I wish I could offer hope. All the tests confirm your cancer has spread to the point where any available treatment would prove ineffective in my opinion. I'm sorry to have to be the bearer of such news, but..." She paused briefly, and continued, "I recommend you talk with your family, get your affairs in order, see your attorney, and arrange nursing care. You also need to make the other necessary arrangements.

I could only manage, "Thank you, Doctor." I walked out of the office, my legs spongy.

Dr. Williams remained at her desk and seemed sad. I remember wondering about that as I left her office.

My mind was in a hazy turmoil as I headed down the hall toward the elevator. Dr. Williams's words were grim. I entered the elevator but had difficulty looking at the two people there who smiled at me. I only hoped they said nothing. To speak would have been difficult. The walk from the elevator to the parking lot on spongy legs seemed an exhausting marathon.

In a trance-like state I found my car, sat in the driver's seat, closed the door, and inserted the key. Then I lost it. "God, why is this happening to me? I've been handed my death sentence."

Sobs racked my body. I know I shouted a few curse words, each word punctuated with my hands hitting the steering wheel. I had no control over this situation, and I don't like having no control.

A young man walking past my car, an arm in a sling, and a bandage around his forehead, looked at me and yelled, "Are you okay? Need any help?"

I looked up, managed to shake my head no, and mouthed, "I'm okay." I waved the guy away, but he probably knew I wasn't okay. No, nothing would likely be okay again.

I reached for a cigarette, but I had none. A cigarette might calm my nerves. But I'd given up the habit years ago. How could I momentarily forget?

She'd told me, "You can't smoke with a baby in the house. I'll not allow it." I didn't put up a fight. I'd loved her and the baby too much. Going cold turkey was hard. Staying busy, sucking on hard candy, and a peaceful house got me through the worst.

I've now been tossed on a train roaring recklessly down a bumpy track, no way to get off, and a dark tunnel ahead. I'd experienced the death of loved ones, but this was different. I'd always known I'd eventually die, just didn't expect it so soon. I'd never see Lance married, nor would I ever see or hold my future grandchildren. The thought, The Lord giveth and the Lord taketh away, crossed my mind. It wasn't much comfort at the moment though.

Eventually, I calmed somewhat. With a tremor, I started the car, my mind still in turmoil. I drove out of the parking garage, headed for Malibu and home.

In the coming days, other unwelcome tasks have been thrust in my path, nursing care arrangements, funeral arrangements, notifying friends, Lance, and my sister. I had no choice. Life had finally thrown me the last of the lemons. Mom had always told Alex and me, "Make lemonade when life hands you lemons." I couldn't help chuckling at the thought. This wasn't going to be lemonade, nor could I add any sweetener.

I drove on through Santa Monica and entered the Pacific Coast Highway. To redirect my mind, I inserted a CD, the <u>Les Miserables</u> London cast album. The music soothed me at that moment. Soon, I was aware of the lyrics. Beautiful music it was, certainly more beautiful than I felt. At that moment, I'd wished I were Jean Valjean. A character in that play, in any play, would be preferable to this anguish.

As expected, I found Mona in the kitchen having coffee. "Mona, could I have a cup of coffee? I'll be out on the patio."

In a few minutes, I had coffee in hand. I sipped slowly, savoring every sip. There would shortly come a time when I couldn't do this. I sipped and made some decisions. I knew everyone, except the public, had to be told. This was not something I looked forward to doing but a required necessity.

I looked toward the ocean recalling the day Erin and I had spent hours on the beach building sand castles with six-year old Lance. I wiped the tears away with the back of my hand. Why the tears? My own death wasn't the worst thing I could contemplate. I found it easier to think about my own death than that of a loved one. Erin's death had been difficult enough. I found it difficult to be leaving all I loved. I suppose the most difficult aspect of facing death is thinking about leaving all that is beautiful and good on earth.

Through my tears, I'd noticed the roses lining the patio, planted so long ago by Erin. It was her garden. Erin's Rose Garden! I rose, walked through the bushes, and leaned down to smell a red rose, Erin's favorite. Memories of her flooded my mind. Walking among her roses always did that.

Devin's Journal, Sunday, April 19, 1992

Before my plane landed in Tucson yesterday morning, my thoughts lingered on Lance and the news I had to tell him. Could I tell him everything?

How he's changed over the years. Our sweet little guy was now a man, about to graduate from the university. His eyes, a brilliant blue, his dimples, and his still-blond hair always fascinated Erin and me. Sally Anne had been accurate—he looked like our biological son might have looked.

Lance had always been smaller than his classmates, and maintained his baby face, accentuated by his longish haircut, until his freshman year in high school. Then he'd begun to transform into something quite different. He began to part his hair and kept it at a shorter length. His face took on a leaner, more chiseled look, the dimples more pronounced. As he neared his senior year, he'd reached his full height.

Having had a few movement classes at the university and some at the studio, I always found it strange that Lance moved with the gracefulness of a dancer, but he wasn't much of a dancer. Looking at him one might have concluded he was never much of an athlete, even though he was 6'1" and packed 165 pounds, yet Erin and I, and all those with whom he had attended high school, knew he was a good tennis player and a track star.

Lance became a fine pianist after years of lessons, but he seldom displayed his talent in public, preferring to play for his own enjoyment or for family and trusted friends. What did he fear? Rejection? He never enjoyed public performances as had been my inclination.

I was amused and periodically annoyed that Lance was such a casual dresser. Lance shared that with Erin who'd also preferred a more casual dress than I.

Lance reluctantly wore the slacks with white shirt and tie required at Saint Paul's but never liked doing so. He preferred shorts and polo shirts worn with sandals or loafers. Socks were taboo except when he was on the tennis court or was required to wear a suit or tux. "Dressing up" to him was slacks, sports coat, and either a tee shirt or open-collared shirt worn with loafers and, of course, no socks. What was his thing about no socks? I never figured that out. On those few occasions when I chided Lance about his attire, Erin would always come to his defense saying, "Dev, he's not in the movies, and he doesn't have a public always looking at him, so stop it."

I learned long ago that Erin never failed to discipline Lance when required, but she always wanted him to make his own decisions. As she always said, "If we don't allow him to make as many decisions as possible, he can never learn to make wise ones." As Lance got older, I saw Erin's wisdom. After all, I married a wise, wonderful, and loving woman.

One of the traits Erin and I most admired about Lance was his honesty. We always attributed that to the time Lance had a problem at Saint Paul's Elementary, his first time being in trouble. During lunch period, he and a number of other boys were caught picking flowers. All the children were taken to Sister Margaret who asked if they had been picking the flowers. Lance was the only one who admitted he had been. For being honest, Sister Margaret sent him back to his classroom. The other children were paddled. This lesson in honesty must have made a deep impression on him, and he never seemed to forget that honesty pays.

When my plane landed in Tucson, I grabbed my carry-on, headed for the gate, and a waiting Lance. His girlfriend was with him. I saw her as soon as I entered the gate area. It was good to finally meet her.

We had a wonderful visit, but I couldn't bring myself to tell him about his being adopted. I should have. I suppose I'm only going to be able to tell him in a letter. Devin, you're a coward!

My time with Lance was memorable. Hope he felt the same way. I was really tired though on the flight back to LA. The visit was a draining experience.

Devin's Journal, Thursday, April 30, 1992

This morning I woke after another restless evening. I'd had a mild headache deadened with one of those pain killers Dr. Williams had prescribed. I showered, shaved, and went down to the kitchen to have the small breakfast Mona had prepared. She asked, "Devin, did you sleep last evening...get any rest?"

"Well, it wasn't a good evening, but I did get some sleep. Feel okay now, and ready to put this day behind me. Billy, Cliff, and

Rick are coming out at ten. We'll meet in the study. I'd appreciate some coffee then."

Mona left the kitchen to do other household chores. I had a small glass of milk, followed by another pain pill, ate some scrambled eggs, pushed the plate back, and headed for the study with the Los Angeles Times to await the arrival of my business team as I often referred to them. All were good men of the highest integrity, all close personal and social friends after our years together.

I met them at the door upon their arrival. As they shook my hand, Cliff asked, probably as planned for the three of them, "How are you, Devin?"

"Okay. I'm ill, but I read the obituary pages in the Los Angeles Times this morning. Found I wasn't listed yet, so I begin the day quite well, I think." They all seemed bewildered by my statement, but made no comments. I was immensely pleased with myself.

Mona entered as we sat, leaving coffee, grapes, strawberries, and Danish pastries on the side table. She said, "Is that all you fellows need now?"

"I believe it is. Thanks, Mona. Guys, have some coffee, fruit, and rolls, and let's get down to business."

After explaining my health situation they all expressed concern and insisted I attempt to find a treatment plan. They gave up shortly seeing my resolve in seeking no further treatment. I was able to leave those concerns and move on to the reasons I had called them to the house.

I directed Billy to cancel everything on my schedule by saying I was experiencing health problems and undergoing medical treatment.

Cliff would continue to pay all bills, put the ranch in Redding on the market, and arrange for in-home nursing care after consulting Dr. Wray.

Rick would make changes to my will, Mona and Ginny would continue to use the guest house for the balance of their lives and Christine was to share the estate with Lance, except Lance would receive the Malibu house, Christine the Santa Monica apartment, and both would share in the proceeds when the Tucson house was sold. . Adding Christine as an heir took Rick by surprise. Billy and Cliff didn't get involved in that discussion, but did have raised eyebrows. Neither said anything, nor did they ask any questions for which I was grateful. Rick agreed to bring the codicil to the will out tomorrow for my signature.

"And finally," I said after accomplishing all I'd intended and needing another pain pill, "I know you will assist Lance if and when he needs anything. Guys, thanks for your friendship over the years. I can't begin to express how much. I've treasured our friendship. I love you guys." Tears began to run down my cheeks. "I'll keep in contact as long as possible."

I stood, embraced each of them, and we walked together to the door, tears also in all their eyes. I'm certain they knew, just as did I, this was not the end of friendship, but likely the beginning of memories and the last time we'd be together. We all knew a friendship never died; it lived on in hearts and memories.

I stood in the doorway and watched their cars fading as they rounded the last curve in my driveway. It seemed as though I was watching years of my life rapidly vanish down the driveway. Having to leave family and friends and all I loved was difficult, likely the worst aspect of death.

Chapter Four

When I arrived back at the house, Aunt Alexa met me at the front door. She drew me into a warm embrace.

"Lance, I'm so glad to see you. Alice told me you were going to visit your mom."

"Good to see you also. Thanks for being here with Dad…and with me. I know Alice thought that was a strange way of putting it, but I always visit Mom when I'm home."

"I understand, but your comment surprised her. She knew your mom had died. Let's go into the kitchen and have some coffee. Mona's been keeping coffee available."

"Sounds good to me."

As we moved towards the kitchen Alex said, "Devin's still sleeping. He's not awake much, and when he is, he's not always coherent. That's been the case for the last week. His pain is severe at times, so he gets heavy doses of pain meds."

"I should have come home a few weeks ago."

"Lance, you know that would have agitated your father, and agitation he didn't need."

"But I needed to come home."

"I understand. Maybe you'll get that visit yet. Sit at the table, and I'll get the coffee."

She returned with our coffee and sat beside me.

"How's Dad really?"

"According to Alice, he's failing quickly. His time's very short, she thinks. I'm sorry to have to give you bad news, but Devin had been anxious to have you home a week ago. He's rapidly gone downhill since. Perhaps he'll wake enough to talk."

"I hope so."

"Did Alice tell you about your Dad's journals and your Mom's diaries on his desk?"

"Yes. I saw them before I left for the cemetery. Even read the first entry of Dad's. Did you look at them?"

"No. They were left for you."

"You know, Alex, Dad never said much about his life prior to coming to California to make his first film. Reading about his life was rather interesting. So he was named after one of grandmother's old boyfriends?"

"Where did you get such an idea?"

"From Dad's journal. He mentioned he had once asked grandmother where his name came from, and she told him he was named after an old boyfriend. Is that true?"

"I don't know, but probably it is if Mom said so. I've never heard that though. I was named after my Uncle Alexander."

"Dad mentioned that in his journal. Guess he had a rather rocky relationship with Grandfather. Did you know about that?"

"No, not until I came out to visit Devin a few weeks ago. He told me about it, but I'll tell you what he said later. Now, why don't we go up and see if Devin's still sleeping?"

Dad was sleeping but moving around periodically. Alex sat in the recliner next to Dad's bed. I pulled the other recliner to the other side of the bed and sat. I touched Dad's hand and told him I was there, but there was no response. I found it difficult to just look at Dad lying in that bed when I wanted to talk with him.

After a few minutes, I told Alex I was going down to the study to read some more of Dad's journals.

Opening the first journal a few minutes later I continued to read.

Monday, March 9, 1959

Journal, my friend,

I need a friend. Today hasn't been one of my better days. In fact, today became a disaster. Downhill it went. Quickly! Shortly after I entered the theatre building lobby this morning, the department secretary met me.

"Devin, a young lady left this with me on Friday afternoon and asked me to give it to you this morning."

"Who was she?" I asked as the secretary handed me the letter.

"I don't know. Never recall seeing her before."

"Thanks."

I turned, walked outside, and opened the envelope. I checked the sender at the bottom of the second page. I was mystified having not conversed with Anna since our parting before Christmas, about eleven weeks earlier, although I'd said "hello" as I'd passed her a few times on campus. I read the letter.

I didn't know what to make of Anna's letter. She'd quit school and was flying home. She mentioned a "wonderful gift" I left her. What could that be? Only one thing came to mind, but I dismissed the thought. Knowing Anna, she would have told me about that. I'm certain. She'd have used it to hang on to me. Surely she didn't *want to torment me? The rest of my day passed in a fog. I found it impossible to concentrate during my classes. And as I think about bed, I just want to sleep. But can I? I have a big test in the morning.*

What was this all about? Did this mean what I thought? Could it be that Dad has another child? I need to ask Alex if she knows about Anna. A few entries later I came to some entries about Mom.

Wednesday, September 10, 1962

Wow. What a day this has been. This morning, as usual, I stopped by the Student Union for coffee before walking on over to the theatre building for my first class. After paying for my coffee and turning around to find a seat, I noticed this girl and a dark-haired, handsome fellow sitting at a table. She was what I'd heard someone once say, "Easy on the eyes." I found a table nearby, so I had a clear view of her.

From my vantage point a few tables away was a classic beauty. She had a beguiling face, more beautiful and beguiling when she smiled, and she seemed to smile a lot. My stomach fluttered. Her light blonde hair curled up to shoulder length, a blonde Elizabeth Taylor she seemed. Her sun-belt tan, and Arizona casual dress, sandals, shorts, and a modestly-cut blouse were appealing. Her informal dress only enhanced her beauty, yet there was a simple elegance about her. She was an animated talker and seemed to enjoy her conversation with the fellow across the table from her. Boy, how I wanted to be that guy. She and her friend rose to leave. As she walked out, I noticed her graceful movement. She seemed perfection. Stunning! I had a desire to follow, but knew I couldn't.

For some unknown reason, I kept thinking we shared a destiny. Strange.

Who was she? I'd been on campus for about four years now yet had never seen her.

Luckily for me, she was sitting down front in the lecture hall when I entered my first theatre class about an hour later. Obviously, she's a senior taking a graduate-level course. I sat as close to her as possible. After class, I noticed her dark-haired coffee mate met her. I'm going to meet this girl. I'll just have to get rid of her handsome coffee mate somehow. I'll try to avoid killing him!

Wednesday, December 19, 1962

I introduced myself to her a few months ago in class and now know her name, Erin Kaylee Evans. Nice name, I think. I've invited her to coffee and to a movie, but she refused. I got the feeling she has some problem with me or is in a serious relationship with that coffee mate.

After months of trying to get better acquainted, I've been unable to get past friendly chats. My one consolation, she always called me "Dev." I loved hearing her say it. Erin's "Dev" was a whisper in my ears, or the ripple of a gently, flowing stream. Her 'Dev' was endearing.

This morning after class, I noticed her coffee mate wasn't in sight, so I said to her as she came out of the classroom, "Erin, who's that guy always meeting you after class?"

"Chuck? He's someone I've known since high school in Scottsdale. He's also a member of my church, and we're good friends."

"Is he a boyfriend or what?"

"Dev, he's a good friend, not a boyfriend." The way she said "Dev" melted me again. "I feel safe with him. He's not in theatre."

"You're taking a theatre course. You don't like people in theatre?"

"It's not exactly that."

"What is it then?"

"I plan to teach theatre."

"So you have a problem with those of us who don't plan to teach theatre?"

"No. I have a problem with the Hollywood-actor type."

"I don't understand, Erin."

"Dev, your type scares me."

"How could I possibly scare you? What have I done?"

"Nothing really. I like you. You're fun to talk with, but..." She paused, looking away as though thinking how she'd word what came next. A moment of fear struck me. Then she looked me square in the eyes and said, "I don't want a relationship with a Hollywood hunk."

I was stunned and could only reply, "Who's a Hollywood hunk?"

"You are."

"Me?"

"Yeah. You, Dev."

"You're joking?"

"No, I'm serious."

"You think I'm a Hollywood hunk? Wow. That's a new one. I'm sorry, but I'm stuck with what God gave me."

"Well, I know about Hollywood types."

"You know, Erin, I'm not that type."

"Well, I doubt that'll always be the case in the future. You probably want a professional acting career."

"I do dream about that."

"Well, that lifestyle's not for me. See you around, Dev." She walked away leaving me standing staring at her, unable to think of any intelligent response.

I started to give chase, but decided the time wasn't right. I'll think about how to get to know her better. Over the next few weeks, I'll develop a plan.

At that moment, Aunt Alex entered the study. "Reading more of your Dad's journals, Lance?"

"Yes. The part I just read was about how Dad and Mom met. Dad had briefly mentioned that when he came to Tucson but didn't relate all the details. Have you ever heard Dad mention an Anna?"

"No, I haven't."

"Suppose I'll find her complete story when I read all these journals. Let me read you the next entry?"

January 24, 1963

Well, today was the day I did it. I implemented my plan.

We started rehearsals for <u>Who's Afraid of Virginia Woolf</u>? on Monday. I have the role of Nick, a biology teacher, and Erin has been cast as Nick's mousy wife Honey. Mousy, Erin's not. I've had three nights of being close to Erin in rehearsals. I liked that. Last night's rehearsal was great. She's really good.

So, this morning I implemented "my plan" to get to know Erin better. I hope it works and doesn't backfire in my face because we have weeks of working together on the play.

Erin and Chuck were sitting in the Union this morning having coffee as they usually do most mornings. I walked over to them, handed Erin a book, and said, "Erin, you left this at my house the other day when we were running lines." She just stared at me with the distain one might have for one of those Arizona cockroaches I sometimes find in my kitchen. Man, I got out of the Union quickly. Thank goodness, the director has cancelled rehearsal this evening. She'll have the evening to cool off if I angered her. Friday evening at rehearsal, I'll find out how she took it.

"Does the next entry tell what happened, Lance?"

"Yeah, I think. I'll read it to you?"

Thursday, January 24, 1963

Journal friend,

I certainly didn't expect Erin to come to my house this evening. That took nerve. Was she ever angry! Suppose I deserved it. The evening was a clearing of the air, but it was much more. She finally gave me more information about herself.

She grew up in the Phoenix area. Her parents graduated from the University of Arizona which explains why she's here. After her dad graduated with his business degree, he became a stock broker in Phoenix. He's done well. Her mom has an English degree and began teaching high school in Phoenix. Eventually, her mom got a position in Tempe where she still teaches. She attended elementary and middle school in Phoenix, but moved to Scottsdale the summer before she entered high school. She played tennis and was active in theatre in high school. She and her parents have always been active in church. Plus, I finally got the entire Chuck story.

I asked her, "Did you meet Chuck in church?"

"Yes, but we also graduated from high school together."

"Did you..."

"No, Dev. We never dated. He's always seemed like a brother, my protector more or less."

"Does he see you as a sister or..."

"I don't know. The subject's never been discussed, and I hope it isn't. He's just my friend, nothing more."

"Did you need a protector in high school?"

"No, not really, but when we were juniors, I was cast in a play opposite a popular athlete. All the girls thought the guy was 'drop-dead' handsome. I suppose he was, but his arrogance and self-importance turned me off, so I avoided him. Being cast opposite that guy for ten weeks of rehearsals plus performances was a trying ordeal, but also meant I couldn't avoid him. Chuck was taking a technical theatre course elective that year and worked on the stage crew for the show. He was almost always backstage. About a week before the play opened, Mr. Self-absorbed Handsome, tried to kiss me backstage. I resisted and might have lost the battle had Chuck not stopped him. Chuck was about to deck the guy when the director intervened."

"Bet someone got into trouble."

"No, we had a show to do and couldn't lose anyone. I could hardly wait for the show to end its run."

"So that's what you meant by Chuck being your protector and safe for you?"

"Yeah, it was."

"And this Mr. Self-absorbed Handsome is related to your avoiding me for so long, right?"

"I suppose. Yes. Sorry. But you've made no advances."

Now I know she and Chuck are not an item. To top off the evening, I was allowed to walk her to her dorm.

I walked away from the dorm entrance alcove and let out a yell, earning the stares I received. I ran the three blocks back to my little house. I thought, Devin do you know how lucky you are?

I may have been attracted to a beautiful woman that morning in the Student Union, but I think this is more. In the morning, we have coffee together, just the two of us. No Chuck. Wow.

I'll not get much sleep this evening, I'm afraid.

"Lance, he doesn't say what happened when your mom came over."

"No. I wonder if Mom mentions what happened at Dad's house in her diary."

"Want me to check in her diary for an entry around January 24th?"

"Yes, please do."

Alex rose from the sofa, got the top diary, finally found the entry, and began to read.

Thursday, January 24, 1963

Some evening I've had. One I'll not forget. I entered the dorm, the door closed, and he walked away, back to his little house on Third Street. Never before have I met someone handsome who wasn't also full of himself. That really struck me about him all evening. There's an attraction between us. I feel it.

When he'd left that book on the table this morning at coffee, I was both astonished and angry. I didn't even know where he lived. I was furious with him about the scene that ensued between Chuck and me after he'd left the book and walked away. I contacted some of those who knew Devin and were also working on the <u>Virginia Woolf</u> production and got his address. That shocked him, I'm sure. He probably didn't think I could discover where he lived. He now knows I'm also resourceful.

So tonight I knocked on his door. He opened the door, saw me, and smiled. His smile disappeared quickly once he realized I was angry. I yelled, "Do you have any idea what you've done with that insane and childish stunt?"

"Erin, I don't need a loud scene my landlady and the neighbors will overhear," he said a bit too calmly for me. That infuriated me even more.

"I don't care. Let them hear. You deserve it."

"Erin, please come inside. We'll discuss this rationally and calmly."

"Discuss this rationally and calmly? Oh you..." I brushed past him and entered his house. I turned back to him and said, "Now, Devin..."

"Now, Erin, what's the problem?"

"What's the problem? Is that a joke?" I shook the book in his face. "You bring this book, hand it to me when I'm having coffee with Chuck, and say, 'Erin, you left this in my house the other day when we were running lines,' and then walk away. Do you know what Chuck did?"

"I don't have a clue, but I have really high hopes." He smiled wildly. I started to whack him with that little book right across his handsome mug, but he shielded himself with his arm.

"Chuck picked it up, opened it, and saw what you'd written, 'Dear Erin, Let me count the ways. Love, Devin.' That's insane. I never ran lines with you here or anywhere else. Then Chuck noticed the book was Elizabeth Barrett Browning's sonnets. Love sonnets! He got up, leaned over, and said, 'I think I make this a crowd.' And he walked out. I've lost a friend. How could you?"

"Erin, I'm sorry, truly sorry, if you've lost a friend. I don't think you will lose his friendship. You've known him too long."

"You're an idiot. He'll never speak to me again."

"I doubt that. He's been your friend forever. You told me he wasn't a boyfriend. I asked for dates; you always said, 'No.' I enjoy talking with you. So, I gave it my best shot."

"Your best shot? Are you nuts, simply arrogant, or what?"

"No, I'm not nuts. I wanted to get to know you. Is that so wrong?"

"Well no, but we're so different, Dev."

"Maybe we're not so different. I know it might come as a big shock to you, a whopping one, but I'm not arrogant. I'm really a rather modest, self-effacing guy."

He seemed sincere, and he'd never really done anything around me which seemed arrogant. At that moment, the thought crossed my mind that maybe I'd been wrong about him.

"Erin, I approached you and got the brush-off. I want to know you better. We have weeks ahead of us working together on this play. Give us a chance."

"I'm not sure, but…" I knew I was weakening. The guy had boyish charm and was so sincere.

"Erin, you'll not regret it. I promise."

I deliberately let that comment hang in the air. He began to fidget. Finally, I said, "Okay, Dev, since we're working together, I'll give it a fair shot over the next few weeks. Maybe I've misjudged you without really getting to know you. You've always been a nice guy."

"Great. It's a deal. Now, how about having a Coke and visiting a bit?"

"Okay, I'll visit a bit."

Devin got two Cokes from the refrigerator, and we sat in his little living room.

I said, "Okay, I want to hear your story, Dev."

"Want the long version or short one?"

"I'll take the medium one." I couldn't hold back a smile.

I found his personal story rather interesting. He was just an ordinary guy. Hearing he had grown up with a detached father was a bit surprising and jarring. My father had been an affectionate man.

As he seemed to wind down his story, I asked, "What were you like as a kid, Dev?"

He laughed. "I was 'goody two-shoes' growing up. Don't smile. I was a good kid. I was the only son. I was seldom sick. I received high marks in school. I enjoyed approval when it was given. Disapproval and a guilty conscience were abhorrent to me. Some might have called me a 'closet imp,' I suppose. I was well-liked, even though not a popular kid. My interests were so diverse from those of my peers. Sports, especially contact sports, were not on my horizon. So here I am, about six months from getting my master's degree in theatre, and then it's out into the big, cruel acting world. Now, I want to hear about you, Erin."

After I gave him a brief story of my life, I noticed it was dark outside. "It's dark now, Dev. Want to walk me to the dorm?"

"Are you kidding? Of course I do."

Walking across campus, he reached for my hand; I clasped his tightly. I felt safe.

At the dorm door, he took both my hands, looked at me, and said, "I'm sorry I upset you. That probably was idiotic stunt. I'm happy to be working with you. It's been a fun evening. Thanks."

"Yeah, it's been fun, Dev. And that was an idiotic stunt." I couldn't help laughing. "But it got my attention. How about coffee in the Union at 7:30 in the morning before my first class?"

"I'd love to have coffee with you every morning."

I chose to ignore that comment and just responded, "Dev, thanks for the evening and walking me to my dorm."

"Oh, you're welcome, Honey."

"Honey?"

"Yeah, Honey. Remember, you're cast as Honey, and I'm your husband Nick." He smiled broadly. "See you in the morning." He walked away, and I entered the dorm.

The "Honey" bit gave me a startle, but thinking about it now makes me laugh. He's a sweet guy. I like him a lot. Never thought I would. I hope he likes me as well. Off to bed and sweet dreams of Dev. Could I be that lucky?

"Lance, now that's an interesting approach to begin a romance. A juvenile soap opera, I think, but they were both young."

"Yeah. I can't believe Dad used a book of poetry, but Dad was probably obsessed with Mom."

"Well, it's strange and unique."

"I'll say. Let's go check on Dad?"

Nothing had changed. He was still sleeping. Alice was with him checking his vitals. I told Alex I was going for a walk on the beach before it got too dark.

Chapter Five

Erin's Diary, Sunday, April 14, 1963

After church this morning, Dev and I packed a lunch and headed for Mount Lemmon, our usual Sunday ritual, lunch from a sack but under the pines.

About half way up the mountain, I noticed there was no <u>Los Angeles Times</u>. I turned to Dev and said, "You forgot the <u>Times</u> today."

"Didn't forget. I just didn't bring it."

"Why not?"

"You'll see later."

"Okay, Dev, what's up?"

"Wait until we get to a picnic table."

Once we had found a table, put our lunch on it, I said, "Okay, tell me now."

"Well, the reason I wasn't available yesterday is that I drove to Scottsdale and had lunch with your parents."

"And you didn't take me?"

"Well, we had a nice lunch and an interesting conversation."

"About what?"

"I asked their permission to marry you."

"You what? And their answer was?"

"They said, 'Yes.' Said they welcomed me into the family, glad I was a Christian, but had concerns about my acting career."

"Yeah, they have said all that to me before. Well, Dev?"

"I promised you many weeks ago I'd tell you about Anna. Not that I want to, but you have to know."

"I'm listening."

"Anna and I dated for about three months. One evening became one of the major regrets of my life. I ended the relationship quickly. I just hope you can forgive me."

"Have you seen her since?"

"I saw her a few times on campus after we broke up. Just said, 'Hello,' and went on my way. Abruptly, she returned home in March of 1959, leaving me a letter."

"And what did it say?"

"She basically said goodbye, but there was a puzzling statement in it about my leaving her a 'wonderful gift.' Plus, she asked me not to contact her and said she'd contact me someday."

"And what was that gift, Dev?"

"I don't know. At first, I thought she might be saying she was pregnant, but I decided were that what she was talking about, she'd have used it to hang onto me and wouldn't have flown home. She's never contacted me, and I question whether she ever will. That's all I can tell you. I'm so sorry to spring this on you now. I'll show you her letter the next time you're at the house. Okay?"

"Why have you kept the letter?"

"In case she contacts me again. It has nothing to do with any feelings for her. There weren't many deep feelings to begin with, but she was interesting. I liked her but didn't love her. You're the first girl I've ever loved. I know this may be difficult for you to understand, and I'm placing you in a dreadful position. You can send me away if you want."

I didn't say anything for a few moments. Dev became uncomfortable, looking around as though seeking a refuge. I responded from my heart, "You know, Dev, unless one walks in another's shoes, one never fully understands." He looked at me with interest. "There've been many times when that's proven difficult, and this is one of those times." I paused. I know the silence frightened Dev. His hands were into his arm pits, and he seemed to hug himself tightly. Then, I said, "I love you Dev. Your past is between you and God. The subject is now forgotten." Dev noticeably relaxed.

After a bit, he said, "Thanks for being the special person you are. You may not feel that way, Erin, if Anna ever contacts me again."

"That might prove difficult, but we'll face the future together and deal with what comes our way. The past is the past, both yours and mine. Let's leave it that way. It's our future we need to talk about. Now, you were saying..."

Dev got down on one knee and looked up at me. "Erin, I think the script calls for the guy to say about now, 'I love you. I want to spend the rest of my life with you. Will you marry me?'"

"Of course, I'll marry you."

Still on one knee, Dev continued, "Erin, what comes next in the script is this." As he stood he reached in his pocket and handed me a white velvet box. "Please open it."

I opened the little box and found a folded note where a ring should have been. "Read the note, Erin." Dev was smiling broadly.

"Dear Erin, I'll spend the rest of my days counting the ways I love you. I know you expected to find a ring here, but when I was looking at rings, I discovered that I didn't really like the traditional wedding band and engagement diamond. Instead, I preferred what's called a cocktail ring. I hope you will not be disappointed with what I purchase. On our wedding day, I think the ring will please you. All my love, Devin."

"Dev, that's so sweet. I can wait for the ring. If someone asks why I don't have an engagement ring, I'll just say, 'Dev can't afford one now.'" I laughed and threw my arms around him and planted a kiss on his lips.

He backed up and said, "Wow!"

Devin's Journal, Saturday, May 4, 1963

I had little clue about what to expect with the screen test. I'd had no university film courses, no exposure to film acting or the needed technique, although I'd watched some filming out at the Old

Tucson Studio. Almost all my training focused on theatre acting. I'd spent a few unsettled weeks before flying to Los Angeles for the screen test Billy had arranged.

Finally, last Thursday morning, I flew to the coast. Billy met me at LAX, dropped me off at the hotel, gave me a script to study, returned in the early evening, took me to dinner; then I settled in, script in hand to finish memorizing lines, and fell asleep around eleven, exhausted.

I rose early the next morning, showered, shaved, dressed, and went down for breakfast. Then back to my room for more line review.

Billy arrived around 9 a.m., and we headed out. After entering the studio gate, Billy drove to a building where he left me to get into costume and have the makeup artist prepare me for the camera. After that, I was taken to the sound stage. Billy awaited me.

Following introductions to the assembled crew, I met the director of From the Brink of Hell who explained what was to occur. As a novice, I was grateful for the explanation and advice. After two run-throughs, the camera rolled.

Being such a film novice, only the director's call, "Cut. Print." told me it was over. After I said "thank you" to all involved, Billy and I walked to the car.

"Devin, it went well," Billy said as we left the sound stage. "A meeting has been called for 5:00 p.m. this afternoon to screen the test. I'll be there. As soon as I have news, I'll come up to your room."

Around 7:30 p.m. that dreaded, yet eagerly anticipated, knock came on my hotel room door. I opened the door to a smiling Billy who entered saying, "Well, kid. They loved it. The role is yours if you want it."

"They liked me?" I was surprised. "So, what's next, Billy?"

Devin's Journal, Monday, May 13, 1963

I signed the movie contract yesterday morning, and Billy became my agent. After lunch, I caught my flight back to Tucson to tell Erin the good news in person.

Erin was at the gate waiting when I came down the ramp. I embraced and kissed her, and as she pulled away came the awaited question, "Okay Dev, how did it go? Spill it."

"Honey, I'll tell you after I get my bag and we're in the car."

As soon as we were in the car, I told her about the screen test, the contract, the filming schedule, and asked, "What do you think?"

"It's a bit scary, but you have my support."

"With my filming schedule, we wait until the movie has wrapped, and then we get married. Let's do it around Christmas? Okay?"

"That's fine with me, and I'm sure my parents and yours will agree."

"Erin, what would you think about us getting married in Hawaii? I've always wanted to go there."

"I'd like that. It's a beautiful place. Surely both our families will approve if that's what we want."

Devin's Journal, Tuesday, May 14, 1963

Alyssa and Brad are supportive and helpful, suggesting the Royal Hawaiian on Waikiki. The hotel has a beach area where we can have the ceremony and then stay around and enjoy an Oahu honeymoon. My parents liked the idea, especially Mom. This would get Dad from in front of the television and to Hawaii.

Erin's Diary, Monday, January 6, 1964

We're back in Tucson now. Had a great time in Honolulu and want to go back someday.

Two days after our wedding we explored Oahu, all the usual tourist spots. A favorite area was the Blowhole, the waves rolling in, striking the rocky shore, sending water shooting through the blowhole creating a wonder of nature. Perhaps it was a favorite spot because to the right of the Blowhole, across the parking lot, we moved to a railing and looked down upon a small beach, Halona Cove Beach, where the Lancaster/Kerr movie From Here to Eternity beach scene had been filmed. Lava-rock formations rose from the small, sandy beach area on three sides. The ocean was to our left, with rock formations below us extending to the small beach and opposite where we were standing. Looking down on the beach and to our right rock formations rose to the coastal highway.

A local standing nearby shared with us information about the small beach. Locals called it Cockroach Cove. We saw no cockroaches. Why cockroach? Some people referred to the beach as Eternity Beach, no doubt because of the movie, while others called it Peering Place. Was that because people like us stood at the parking lot railing peering down at the beach? The lava rocks in and around the beach appeared hazardous, but the local pointed out a trailhead leading down to the beach located next to the Blowhole parking lot entrance off the highway. He said it wasn't dangerous if one were careful.

When we expressed interest in going down to the beach, he told us that in the center of the sandy beach area of the cove was a lava-tube tunnel under the highway leading to the other side. He then warned us that the water was great for swimming when the surf was calm, but there was dangerous swimming if the surf was turbulent. Outside the protected cove area, strong currents were possible and extremely dangerous.

As honeymooners, Dev felt we had to be on that beach where two other screen lovers had spent time.

Dev turned to me. "We have to come back here after dark tonight and create our own beach scene."

"That'd be fun, but it looks treacherous."

"Let's use the trailhead and check it out. It'll be a less dangerous in daylight and good practice for after dark."

We made our way down slowly, the local and other tourists watching in surprise. They thought we were a bit mad, no doubt. We probably were.

After our practice climb down and back up, we returned to the hotel.

Following dinner that evening, we drove back to the Blowhole parking lot. The moonlight created dancing white caps on the rolling waves as we drove along the highway above the ocean,.

There were no cars in the parking lot. We liked having the beach to ourselves. The moonlight cast sufficient light on the rocks so our previously chosen path down was visible, assisted by the flashlight we had brought along. Holding onto rocks and carefully placing our feet, we descended to the beach level.

About halfway down, I said, "This wasn't easy during daylight. Tonight, this seems really crazy."

We both laughed. Dev responded, "Yeah, it's a bit crazy, but the adrenaline rush and you make it doubly exciting."

The waves coming ashore at the beach level appeared a bit menacing with the moonlight hitting them, more menacing than they appeared from the highway. We stripped to our swim suits and placed our clothing and shoes on the rocks, out of the waves' reach.

Much like little kids, we ran, hand in hand, into the water, staying close to shore.

After a brief swim we lay on the beach, the cool waves washing over us, reminiscent of the movie scene.

As we dressed later, Dev chuckled, and turning to me said, "You're beautiful in the moonlight. I think we should be glad there wasn't a Hollywood film crew around tonight."

I couldn't help laughing. "If cameras had been around, I'm sure our pictures would be on the gossip pages. And you're not bad in the moonlight either."

"Maybe a magazine story and pictures of us is the publicity my movie needs."

"Perhaps, but I think we should be happy to be spared that drama."

Devin's Journal, Tuesday, January 7, 1964

My first movie, <u>From the Brink of Hell</u>, wrapped two weeks before Christmas. Since I had my first film earnings, I had bought Erin's ring in Hollywood before I flew back to Tucson.

Three days after Christmas, Erin and I flew to Honolulu for our wedding. Her parents had flown over to make the final arrangements the day after Christmas. My parents and Alex had flown over from Oklahoma City to help out.

I vividly recall waking the morning after the wedding. I saw daylight around the window drapes before rolling over to see the clock read ten o'clock. I'd been unable to sleep that late for months with my filming schedule. I turned back, propped on my elbow, head in my hand, and looked down at my beautiful Erin. For the rest of our lives there would be mornings such as this. The sheer joy of being with someone you love, on that morning especially, won't ever be forgotten. Yes, Erin had been my destiny.

I reached over and brushed the hair off Erin's face. She opened her eyes, looked up, smiled at me gazing at her, and said, "And what are you thinking, dear husband?"

"Maybe you don't want to know, dear wife."

"Oh, I bet I do."

"Well, for one thing, I was thinking how blessed I am to have you in my life."

"Dev, the feeling is mutual."

Oahu is a wonderful place to enjoy a honeymoon. We'll get back here often.

Devin's Journal, Sunday, January 26, 1964

We've had busy weeks since Hawaii.

After our honeymoon, we flew back to Tucson and my little house to begin married life and await the release of <u>From the Brink of Hell</u>. Fortunately, the Hollywood buzz created by first-cut screenings of <u>Brink</u> enabled Billy to secure contracts for me to appear in two other back-to-back films, the first to begin shooting in February. Erin and I decided a film career was possible. It was time to give up the little house in Tucson.

A week ago, we moved to the West Coast and rented an apartment in Santa Monica. The apartment's an easy commute to the studio for me, and a short distance from a number of schools where Erin hopes to substitute teach until she can find a high school theatre position in the fall.

Our apartment's two blocks from a large non-denominational church which has a young minister, Sam McDonald. On our first visit this morning we liked the church and the minister and decided this would be our church home.

I've reconnected with my San Jacinto pals from elementary school. How they have changed. But I've changed also. When I had mentioned to my film colleagues I needed a lawyer and an accountant/business manager, my old friends Cliff and Rick, were recommended. Rather unusual, I thought. Naturally, both have changed since we were kids, but so have I.

Cliff Dunne, now my accountant and business manager, is a tall, trim, athletic guy who plays tennis regularly. He is careful with his weight, closely monitoring his eating habits. He's now a stylish dresser, but he can afford to dress well. His clients are some of the highest paid people in the entertainment business.

Rick Montgomery agreed to become my attorney. I needed one. There were just too many legal papers to sign and without advice one would have problems. Rick now seems sort of an enigma to many. Beneath his seemingly rough, brusque demeanor, is a kind-hearted man, hidden from all who don't know him well. His always-shined shoes appear in stark contrast to his slightly, rumpled appearance. His suits never seem to retain that well-pressed look for some unknown reason. Rick is now going bald. I've been told the uninformed think of him as a little-talented lawyer; yet the informed know him to be a sought-after, highly talented attorney who has his own Los Angeles legal firm.

I'm lucky to have them working with me, but more important to all three of us is our renewed friendship.

Chapter Six

Wednesday, June10, 1992, Early morning

The conversation with Dad in Tucson was the last I'll have with him. I'm going to miss him. Really miss him. During the last four years the two of us adapted to a life without Mom as best we could. Now I'll have to also adapt to a life without Dad.

Walking along the beach yesterday afternoon, I saw a pigeon land on the wet sand, seeking food, no doubt. Similarly, I had landed at LAX days ago anticipating some meaningful moments conversing with Dad. I met a different Dad than the one who had flown to Tucson weeks before to tell me his cancer was terminal.

About six weeks after Dad's consultation with his specialist, his health had begun to dramatically worsen. The fatigue, weakness, headaches, and chest pain intensified, and his weight loss increased. Alexa had been staying with him for over four weeks by the time I arrived home. The loyal and obedient son had remained at the university until his graduation. I regret not being disobedient this one time. Why was I always obedient? Did I fear something? Rejection maybe?

I know becoming dependent--losing mobility and control over his body—had concerned him after he received his death sentence. Dad was that way; he always liked to be in control. He knew his life was ebbing; his time was near.

Alice, his nurse, had told me after I arrived home that Dad had been only concerned with living long enough to spend some time with me. He needed to talk with me he had told her. I wondered why. We'd recently been together in Tucson. Was there something he hadn't told me? Talking with me consumed him; it kept him fighting Alice thought. But she also thought the fight in him was now almost exhausted.

By the time the nursing staff came on board full-time, Dad's condition had deteriorated to the point he rarely got out of bed, yet he had lucid moments. He was drifting in and out more often. My once strong, active, vibrant Dad had become almost a shell.

Alice had called Dad, Devin, per his instructions when she came as part of the nursing staff responsible for his final weeks of in-home care. And, of course, she was Alice to him. Dad preferred that sort of informality.

One morning about two weeks ago, she told me she'd noticed Dad appeared concerned, worried. "How are you this morning, Devin?" she'd asked. "Is something bothering you?" He nodded yes.

He weakly responded, "Not eating much now, tiring quickly, easily. Want to make plans…a trip."

Alice told me she'd often heard similar statements from previous terminal patients. They must have some sense, or God gives it to them, they're nearing death. For some that awareness can be comforting, the pain and discomfort will soon end. For others, there is a feeling they have things left undone, dreams unfulfilled, relationships needing reconciliation, doubts about what the death experience might be like.

"So Devin, you're planning on taking a trip?" She'd asked him.

"Alice, I want to return to…" He never told her where. He paused briefly and then continued, "Erin and I…not sure I feel like it though."

"Devin, are you perhaps talking about leaving, but not to some place you've been before, maybe a different kind of trip? Perhaps about dying?"

He slowly nodded yes, opened his mouth to speak, paused, but then said nothing more.

"If that's the trip you mean, you don't have to worry…I'm wondering if you'd like me to explain death based on my observations as a nurse."

He nodded yes again, smiled sadly, and said, "Yes. Need to be ready."

"Devin, the usual pattern follows this course. In your case, I think it will be much the same…. You will continue to become weaker…at some point possibly weak enough so that movement and talking may be difficult…maybe weeks before or days or hours." She had paused often, she said, ascertaining he understood and that this was the information he was seeking before continuing. "You may reach the point where you cannot swallow pain pills…injection, suppository, or liquid under your tongue will then be used…but any pain you might experience will be controlled, you will be at ease… eventually your breathing will slow, become soft and quiet, and then cease."

"Will I have pain?"

"No. You'll likely move into warmth, light, be peaceful…none of this should cause pain or fear…then you will go quietly home to Jesus and Erin." Thankfully, Alice knew Dad was a religious person and would find her comments comforting.

He smiled weakly and said quietly, "Thanks." Then he drifted into a peaceful sleep.

Another morning, about twelve days ago, Alice said as she took Dad's vitals, he'd weakly said, shortly after she came on duty, "Had dream last night, Alice."

"Want to discuss it with me, Devin?" No response came for a minute or so while he must have pondered whether to share.

Finally, hesitantly, he began, "I was on the beach…out there…camera…filming two people walking…talking, holding hands…"

"Do you know who they were?"

"I think one was me…the other Erin…we parted…turned… walked in opposite directions…along the beach…after a few steps, we each turned back and faced the other, she extended her arm and hand…reaching for me, beckoning, and then said, 'See you, Dev…' Everything faded."

"Do you know what your dream means?"

"I'd…be seeing her?"

"Did the dream and what you saw scare you, Devin?"

"No. Felt good. Wanted to join her, but woke up." A few minutes later he fell back asleep.

Dad passed away early this morning, a perfect California beach day, slightly breezy, sunny. Perfect in all ways, except one. Alexa had called me a few days ago at Alice's suggestion. The end was very near, at the most, days had been her professional medical opinion.

Alle had taken me to the Tucson airport after my graduation where I caught my flight to LAX.

I had rushed into the house and into Dad's bedroom early that afternoon, four days ago. Four days with an unresponsive Dad. I know Dad thought he'd live long enough to have time with me after the graduation, but as with other cancer patients Alice had served in the past, she said that even medical professionals are unable to make definitive predictions, and patients definitely aren't. Cancer is simply not accommodating.

After my first day home, I spent hours at Dad's bedside talking to him, but he seemed unresponsive. If he heard me, there were no indications. He stirred periodically when Alex or I would speak to him as though he wanted to respond, struggled to do so, but couldn't. We remained close at Dad's bedside during the last three days, and slept in the two recliners Dad and Mom had always used when watching a late movie.

This morning Dad had been restless since daylight. He seemed on the verge of waking. Alice had told us that she thought the end was near, that his hearing would be the last to go, so talk to him. Alexa and I were sitting on either side of his bed. We each held one of Dad's hands. I found it painful to see him that way, but I could do nothing. As his breathing became more labored and strange, I said the words once again. They were broken by my choking sobs, "I'm here Dad…Wake up…Graduation's over…I did it…I love you…Don't leave me now…I need more time with you."

For what seemed liked minutes, but perhaps only a few seconds, there was no response. Then Dad's eye lids fluttered, finally remained open, focused on me. He appeared to recognize me, the hint of a smile forming. Haltingly, almost inaudibly, he said, "So…sorry…love you…Lance…Forgive me… need to tell you…Christine…" He momentarily seemed to gasp for breath, then weakly added…"adopted…" He said no more, his strength gone. His eyes closed, opened again briefly, and appeared to focus on me; the beginning of a real smile came. I wondered if he were seeing Mom and Jesus. Then he just seemingly drifted into sleep. A few seconds later, his breath ceased, then started again, and finally he took one deeper breath, his last.

I remember crying out, "Dad, don't leave me…We need time." Then I rested my head on his lifeless chest.

*****

As I continued walking along my favorite stretch of Pacific sand, gentle waves washed over my feet. Unlike times when I was younger, my troubles didn't wash out to sea. They lingered.

I sat on a familiar rock, feet from the shore line, as the waves rolled in. The calm I'd usually experienced on the beach eluded me, buried by thoughts of Dad still on his bed up at the house.

I had remembered so many thoughts as they rolled through my mind while Alexa and I had sat at Dad's bedside through those long days and nights, days and nights of his seemingly never-ending goodbye. Shortly after he drew his last breath, I simply couldn't move, my head rested on his lifeless chest, no tears were left to flow, for the sheet across his lifeless chest had long since absorbed all my tears. As I raised my head, I saw the picture across the room.

All my life that picture containing a parchment copy of an Edgar A. Guest poem had hung on my parents' bedroom wall. Dad had read the poem to me once many years ago when I was in upper elementary school.

I remember inquiring about the poem in my teens. Dad told me it had three titles, "A Child of Mine," "To All Parents," and "God's Lent Child." The poem had first been published in a newspaper about eight years before Dad was born. It appeared in a collection of Guest poems entitled "Living the Years" in 1949, but I hadn't read the collection as Dad suggested. I recall asking Dad if Guest was a famous poet. His reply: "Not really, but I liked his work."

By the time I was in high school, I knew the death of a child was a highly traumatic event because one of my friends had lost a baby sister. Was a child's death worse than a parent's? How could what I was currently experiencing be worse?

Since then, each time I'd read the poem, I always found most interesting the idea that God lends us children, and we must understand if they leave us early. Could one really understand that kind of loss? What special meaning could that poem have had for Mom and Dad? They surely hadn't lost a child. Or had they? Who was this Christine Dad had mentioned? A lost daughter?

I'd always wondered the poem's significance, but neither Dad nor Mom ever gave my queries further explanation. Instead, their faces registered pain, especially Dad's, and they either changed the subject or moved away. I'd often wondered why. What was the mystery of the poem?

I don't recall how long I'd stayed at Dad's bedside, but eventually Aunt Alex came back into the room, stood behind me, and touched my shoulder to console me. Not her touch or much of anything else could console me at that moment.

She said, "Lance, Alice has made all the phone calls. Someone will be here soon to get Devin. Let's go down to the patio."

"Aunt Alex, I need some alone-time. I'm going down to walk along the beach."

"I'll be here when you get back. We can talk then if you want."

"I'd like that."

There was an unreality about all this. I felt it, but I knew deep down it was all too real. My father was up there on the bed. He may have appeared to be only sleeping; the reality was that he was gone, never to return. This was my reality at the moment. I did have Alex. Even though she was my aunt, I really didn't know her well for some reason I'd never understood.

I walked downstairs, out onto the patio, across the yard, and through the gate leading down to the beach. I removed my shoes once I reached the sand. The sand, its warmth while pleasant, wasn't the warmth of Mom and Dad. The sand had a harshness, not the gentleness of my parents. Dad's last words "Christine" and "adopted" troubled me.

As I looked at the ocean, the waves washing ashore, they seemed a regular beat, the eternal Pacific heartbeat. My father's heartbeat was no more.

Chapter Seven

Wednesday, June 10, 1992, Morning

As I had sat on the rock in the sand remembering Dad's last days, I watched the waves coming ashore, generating a myriad of happy memories of our family together on the beach, in this very spot. If only I had come home as I'd wanted, perhaps I'd have had time to talk with him. I knew I'd always regret that. Were "Christine" and "adopted" really his last two words? Those words troubled me. How were they related to me? Perhaps Alex knew. Maybe I had not heard correctly.

During my time on the beach, they came and took Dad's body. I never even asked who they were, the coroner's office or the funeral home. I was relieved it had been done while I was on the beach though. I hope that's not a disrespectful or horrible thing to say, but I simply couldn't have endured watching Dad leaving his house, never to return.

I rose from the rock, my feet sinking in the sand as I carried my shoes and wearily trudged up the path to the gate leading onto our property. As I approached the house, I noticed Aunt Alex sitting on the patio. She turned to see me, smiled, and held my gaze.

I sat next to her at the table, an umbrella shielding us from the sun. I asked, "Aunt Alex, were Dad's last words 'Christine' and 'adopted'?"

"Yes, Lance, I'm sure they were."

"Why? What was he talking about? Is Christine my sister or someone else? Why did Dad say 'adopted'? "

Aunt Alex looked at me without saying a word. I began to think she might not respond. Finally, she said, "Lance, I don't like this. I've never heard him mention a Christine. Perhaps she's someone he knew in college or..." She paused, a pained expression on her face. "Adopted though, I know about. This shouldn't have been left to me, but…what your father was trying to say by 'adopted' is something you should've been told long ago."

"He was talking about me? Adopted? I'm adopted?"

She reached over, took my hand, and said, "Yes, Lance. You were adopted a few days after you were born. Devin intended to tell you, and he would have had he lived long enough. He knew you should have been told long ago."

I felt something stop. My heart? No, it was my breath. Finally, I took a breath. My stomach felt heavy and a bit upset. I momentarily thought I might lose what little was there.

I was stunned and shaken. How could this be? For seconds I sat staring at the stone patio. I might have cried, but there were no tears left to shed. "You knew?"

"Yes, I've always known."

"Why didn't they ever tell me? This is hard to accept. It can't be."

"I'm sorry. I don't really know why you were never told. I can only tell you what your dad told me when he asked me to come out and what I surmise from that conversation."

"What was that?"

"Lance, he probably called me shortly after he'd seen the oncologist. I was out, but he left a message to call him. He must've been close to the phone when I returned his call because he answered quickly. We talked briefly before I realized something was wrong. After my questioning about what was wrong, Devin admitted he had cancer. I was devastated and agreed to fly out."

"Aunt Alex," I said interrupting her, "we were together in Tucson. Why didn't he tell me? Are you sure I'm adopted?"

"Yes, I'm sure. And he should have told you. You know, Lance, I hadn't had a conversation on the phone with Devin that lasted that long in ages. I think he felt all alone. It hurt to know he was seriously ill. There's no way I could have refused his request to come out."

******

Devin was on the couch in the study when Mona led me in. She said, "Would you like coffee?"

"No coffee, Mona. Not now, perhaps later. We just need time together," Devin answered.

I walked toward the couch, Devin stood, and I fell into his outstretched arms. He seemed tired. I sensed he felt alone. My tight embrace must have been welcomed because he returned it. If he felt alone, he was alone no longer.

I withdrew from the embrace and said, "Devin, it's great to see you. Now tell me what you didn't say on the phone."

"Alex, there's not much left to tell. I'm ill, terribly ill." *He sat and indicated I sit beside him.*

"How ill are we talking about, Devin? You look tired, but…" He interrupted me.

"I've known for some time it was cancer, but…"

"Why didn't you call me?"

"I thought I'd beat it."

"Surely you can." I said, probably more determined and confident than I felt.

"About two years ago, cancer was found in the upper lobe of my left lung. That lobe was removed. The surgeon thought he got it all. When I had recovered sufficiently, I had two rounds of chemo. That was worse than the surgery."

"But you recovered from that?"

"Only for months it seems. Then a few months ago I began to experience those symptoms again, shortness of breath, coughing, but I also had headaches this time, often severe. My doctor suspected the cancer had returned, so I eventually had tests and scans. The works! A few days ago, I saw the oncologist. The cancer's returned, now in both lungs. In addition, it's spread to the liver and brain. It's inoperable, and there's no treatment which would be successful."

"Oh, Devin, I wish you'd called me earlier." The tears were rolling down my cheeks. "You're the only immediate family I have left. No treatment? Surely there are treatments available today."

"I've had those chemo and radiation treatments, Alex. They didn't work for long, and there's only a slim chance of them working now."

"Well, that's better than no chance. You've talked with Lance?"

"Yes, last Saturday. He also said any chance was better than no chance, but I'm not going through that again. I have no more than four months remaining, if I'm lucky."

"Oh Devin," I reached over and touched his arm, "I'm so sorry." I was sobbing as he put his arm around my shoulders and drew me close. "You have to do some-thing, Devin."

"I'll do nothing more. Nature will take its course, un-less I get a miracle. That's the reason I called and asked you to fly out. I need your help."

"Anything." I said moving out of his embrace and looking at him. "What can I do?"

"I need you to come out as soon as next week, and stay with me."

"Won't Lance be here?"

"No, I've asked him to stay at the university until he graduates. Then when the end comes, I need you to stick around to support him, for as long as he needs you. He has no one else other than Mona, Ginny, and my closest friends. Could you do that?"

"I can close up the house. There's someone who can keep an eye on it."

"Glad you'll be here, especially for Lance. I'll make all the final arrangements with the funeral home, my pastor and the church, and with my attorney and business peo-ple. You and Lance will be spared those tasks. Last Satur-day, I even met Lance's girlfriend, a beauty. She reminds me of Erin. I'll call him every day as long as I'm able, and when I'm not, you can take over. I assured him we would have time after graduation."

"Will you?"

"I'm not sure, but if not, I want you here with him."

"I will be."

"He understands how serious this is, I think. He knows my time is short. I intended to tell him his own story. Just couldn't bring myself to do that after..."

"You and Erin never told him?"

"We always intended to, but..."

"You never... Why didn't you tell him?"

"Not sure. Fear maybe."

*****

"Why?" I interrupted Alex once again, "Why didn't they tell me? This is hard to accept, Alex. Why? Why?"

"Lance, I know it's hard. Let me share your dad's comments about your grandfather."

*****

"Your dad said, 'I know he should have been told, Alex, but by the time we decided to tell him, Dad had committed suicide, and Mom had the heart attack. You dealt with all that alone. We just flew in for the funerals. Then afterward, we still did nothing about telling him.'"

"At least you all came."

"It wasn't easy for me, Alex. All I thought about on the flight out was I'd lost something, something never to be retrieved."

"What do you mean?"

"A chance at a real relationship, remote though it may have been. Dad never understood me. Mom did. Mom often told me she loved me. Dad never did. Not once that I recall."

"Devin, you've never shared that with me."

"I never even told Erin. I found grieving difficult until I was able to shed tears. Those tears didn't happen until after Dad and Mom's funeral, and I was alone here. Now I see my tears were not so much because of Dad's death or the suicide, but for us spending years together without sharing a serious personal relationship. We lived in the same house, yet had never known each other. He was always working, or relaxing in front of the television. As a youngster, I remember wanting to do things with him such as fishing, but he never had time for that. In many ways Dad and I were nothing more than 'strangers passing in the night.'"

"Devin, I'm so sorry. That must have been difficult to deal with alone."

"It was, but looking back on Dad's suicide and my relationship with him, I think my tears were not only a release of emotions, but also my final realization that a personal relationship with my father had now become a permanent loss, a sealed door, never to open again."

"I wish you'd talked with me about all this long ago."

"I couldn't. It's not easy now. I think Dad loved me, but he never told me. That hurt. Still hurts. I knew with Dad's death any chance for a relationship was gone forever. That also played a part in why I never told Lance, I think. We feared he might love us less, or at least I did."

"You know he wouldn't have, Devin."

"I failed Lance in many ways, even though I tried not to. Maybe even Erin too. Not telling Lance was both our failures."

"Devin, you failed neither of them, and you know it. You did your best at the time, but Lance should've been told. He deserved that at a younger age."

*****

"Yes, Aunt Alex, they should have told me. I still can't believe this. I always felt something was missing in my life, and I always feared rejection. Wonder if it's related to my being adopted."

"Lance, I don't know. Rest assured, neither your dad nor your mom failed you, although he may have thought he did. He gave you both affection, unlike your grandfather with Devin and me."

"He did and so did Mom, Aunt Alex, but why didn't they tell me I was adopted?"

"They should have, Lance, but your parents weren't perfect. In fact, your dad used those very words to me. 'Alex,' he said, 'it's awful to realize you're not perfect.'"

I understood intellectually all Aunt Alex had just told me, but still…

I just sat there saying nothing for minutes, my elbows on my knees, my head in my hands. I have to believe it. I'm adopted. They never told me. Why?

Finally Aunt Alex said, "Lance, do you want time alone now or…"

"No. Time alone won't help me. Want to go down and walk on the beach with me? I need to walk there again. Staying here in the house won't help me now. Would you come with me?"

"I will, Lance," she said. "Let me change my shoes."

While Alex was changing shoes, I recalled a World War II vet coming to one of my high school history classes. After he concluded talking about his experiences during the war, one of my friends asked him if the war was the worst experience of his life. His response was, "No, it certainly wasn't. The worst experience was when I entered the service and had to produce my birth certificate. When I asked my parents for it, they had to tell me I was adopted. I had never known or suspected. Why I wasn't told as a youngster, I don't know. I could have handled it better then, I think. I'm still troubled about not being told. I think it has driven a wedge between my parents and me to this day."

I suppose to a great extent I feel like that vet now and wonder why I wasn't told at an early age. I don't think it would have been such a shock then. Even in light of all Aunt Alex had just told me, I was still troubled. No wedge could be driven between me and my parents. At least, I didn't think so. I just needed to understand.

Chapter Eight

Devin's Journal, Tuesday, April 14, 1992

It'd been sometime since Alex and I had seen each other. The last time was at Erin's funeral. Of course, we'd always been in contact over the years, through phone calls and regular holiday cards and presents. I knew it'd been too long. Alex was always my support as a kid. I admired her strength and assertiveness. I called her this afternoon to come out and see me.

Tonight after dinner, I'd also called Lance and asked him to meet me Saturday morning at the Tucson airport. Lance was pleased, but disappointed I'd only stay one evening. He was surprised his Aunt Alex was coming out on Monday. She was almost a faceless aunt to him, best known from letters, Christmas cards, and the gifts she always sent him at Christmas and on his birthday. I'm to blame for that and regret it.

Today was emotionally exhausting. The appointment with Dr. Williams only confirmed what had been nagging at me for the weeks before Dr. Wray had ordered more tests. The chest pain, headaches, and coughing had been my flashback to many of the same symptoms before my lung surgery and the chemo months and months ago. I had wondered silently and prayed for healing, but... There is a reason for all this, but I'm not privy to God's thinking. There will likely be no remission, only deadly tentacles again on the march, quickly, steadily, resolutely, and relentlessly. I'm the soldier off to the battle against, not only a formidable enemy, but one assured of victory. And like the soldier, what am I to do? A soldier can't withdraw; cowardice isn't in his nature, and there's no place to run or hide anyway. I know I too have to march on. This darkness will become light. Isn't darkness always followed by light at some point? I may not see tomorrow in this world though. We're all just passing through, on our way to another life. A better one, I believe.

I remember hearing once that the value of a life isn't in one's accomplishments, but in the impact that life has on others. Other than Lance and Alex, will there be anyone else to remember me or on whom I might have made an impact? Why does that seem so important at this moment? Is it really important that someone remember me? Perhaps not as important as having had a lasting impact on someone.

My eyes fell on the night stand and one of my favorite photos. A friendly tourist had volunteered to take it as Erin, Lance, then about twelve years old, and I had stood near the Arch of Triumph on our last visit to Paris. Only Christine was missing. At the time the photo had been taken, I had thought we'd always be together. You know, "There will always be Paris..."

Devin's Journal, Wednesday, April 15, 1992

This morning, I'd begun my first full day on life support. How else am I to think about my days between now and the end, except using the term "life support"?

I was tired but had no pain this morning. Last evening I had a headache and some chest pain. Dr. Wray had told me both were normal and would probably get worse in the coming weeks. I'd slept well thanks to the pain and sleeping pills until I woke from that dream. The dream had been about Erin, but the details were unclear to me this morning. I lay in bed listening to birds singing happily outside because Mona didn't come in early. How I wish I could muster that sort of happiness at the moment. The nightstand clock read six. I seldom woke at six or earlier unless I had to be on the set for an early call. But I hadn't worked in about two years as I'd secretly battled cancer and gone through treatment. Only Mona and Lance and perhaps Ginny had known my secret, but still it had been a lonely battle. Does everyone in my situation feel this loneliness? I'm looking out at a world swimming in non-cancer victims. I don't fit in the non-cancer world any longer, and I don't think they understand fully a cancer patient's plight.

Few people spend lives in a dream career, one they love. Fewer still have that career on their own terms as has been my fortune. I've been blessed. I know it. I have from a young age had dreams and purpose. Erin and I have also encouraged Lance to have dreams; maybe, that's our major legacy to him. I've lived my dreams. To have lived a life devoid of dreams would have been worse than my current fate. A man with no dreams or purpose is nothing but an empty shell regardless of how he might attempt adorning that shell. My purpose and dreams had included Erin and Lance. How I wish they could have included Christine. I made an effort. Thinking about my life brings a smile, bittersweet though it is. I had fulfilled most dreams, and I can honestly say there aren't too many regrets. Regrets? Reminds me of listening to my favorite recording of Edith Piaf's "No Regrets." Perhaps I should feel more regrets. Is that wrong?

Devin's Journal, Monday, October 2, 1978

I feel as though I've been caught up in some horrible Oklahoma tornado, sucked up, spinning out of control, then roughly thrown into a lonely, isolated farm field, severely wounded.

Alex called over a week ago to say Dad and Mom had both died. No, it wasn't an accident or an illness; Dad had committed suicide, and Mom had had a heart attack soon afterwards.

Erin, Lance, and I immediately caught a flight to Oklahoma City.

The stroke Dad had suffered, and from which he'd almost totally recovered a few weeks later, was no doubt the major factor in his suicide. He must have thought other, and perhaps more debilitating, strokes were to follow. Mom had left to visit a relative for the day. Shortly after seeing Mom leave, their neighbor heard two noises sounding like gun shots from Mom and Dad's garage but didn't follow up on the noise she'd heard. Why, I've wondered. Maybe fear. Dad's first shot never pierced the skull, just grazed the scalp and entered the garage ceiling according to the investigating officers. That first shot must have stunned him. About five minutes later, the neighbor reported hearing a second shot, the one that did the fatal damage. Mom came home later, saw Dad on the garage floor when she opened the door, and called 911. I cannot imagine the horror she experienced. Then she had collapsed of a heart attack. Both were dead when the ambulance arrived.

These past days have been just a nightmare for me. Nothing seems real, but then it's all too real. I just wanted to be alone and cry, but that didn't happen until I returned to Malibu and home.

Erin knew I was suffering in silence and kept asking if I were okay. I couldn't admit to her I wasn't. Then I'd lose control of my emotions.

My relationship with Dad has always troubled me. What relationship I had with him wasn't much. Our film had ended with no resolution. While I found that sad, my mom's death was devastating. She understood me at least. Now only Erin did.

I just wanted to return to work. I wanted my life back, but I guess my life is now different, never to be the same again. I'm a suicide survivor and always will be thanks to Dad.

One of the worst aspects of this situation was overhearing some guy at the reception following Mom and Dad's funeral say that those who commit suicide go to Hell. I thought the comment beyond insensitive; it was cruel, whether I was intended to overhear it or not. Are those who commit suicide rational? Are those who commit suicide, but are believers in Christ before the irrational act, damned to Hell? Isn't God a God of love? Who appointed that guy Dad's judge and jury? These things are God's to judge, I think.

All I really know is that suicide devastates much like a war-time explosion—everyone close is hit with the shrapnel. In the case of suicide, the shrapnel is serious emotional debris which also embeds. Suicide is a war zone, and there are lingering post-traumatic effects on so many. I'm experiencing them.

Chapter Nine

June 1992

As we were walking along the beach later, Alex picked up our previous conversation, "Lance, after Devin and Erin brought you to Oklahoma City for a visit when you were about two, I'm certain they feared something being said to you when you were older."

"So they stayed away?"

"Yes. They probably didn't want you feeling different. In their minds they thought they were protecting you."

"Did my grandparents know I was adopted? Your parents, I mean?"

"Your dad called and told them. But he called back a short time later and told them not to mention it again. As far as I know, they didn't. We never discussed it. Lance, I know Devin and Erin also feared you would love them less if they told you, and…"

"I wouldn't have."

"I know, but his poor relationship with your grandfather was difficult for Devin. Our father never told him he loved him, a pain which always hounded him. Dad and Devin really didn't have a lot in common except genes. Devin's reality was the possible loss of your love if you were told you were adopted, I think."

"Is all of this why I remember only seeing you a few times at funerals, my grandparents', Uncle Dave's, and Mom's?"

"Yes, I think so. I'm sure Devin and Erin felt we might say something accidently."

"You know, I'm more hurt than angry at the moment."

"Lance, this will take time for you to process."

"I know, Aunt Alex."

I simply couldn't muster anger towards my parents for never having told me I was adopted or having never mentioned Christine. Intellectually, I think, I wanted anger, but my heart didn't. Upset, stunned, and disappointed was my state of mind at the moment. My parents loved me. There was no malice behind them never telling me.

I recalled a passage I'd read in Dad's journals:

I've had another day I dreaded. I woke early this morning, no pain, having awakened an hour earlier and taken a pain pill. I was extremely tired. I lay in bed thinking about this feeling of loneliness.

Over the weeks, I've experienced a range of emotions--regret, denial, grief, laughter, fear. They come upon me at various times, unexpectedly. Waves washing ashore, and then ebbing out again, repeatedly. Even with people around who care, I feel loneliness. Do others understand what I'm experiencing? Does everyone who knows they're dying experience this loneliness? I feel I'm on the outside looking in on a group of people without cancer. Regardless of what I do or try, I don't seem to fit in. I can no longer feel a part of the group like I once did. Preparation for the other life? I've pondered that.

I wonder if everyone who knows his life is short has such thoughts. At times, I feel I could use a self-help book, but I've never seen Dying for Dummies in a book store.

I too had experienced a range of emotions since hearing the words "Christine" and "adopted." Regret, denial, grief, and fear will likely be a part of my new existence. Those old feelings of something missing and the fear of rejection returned to haunt me.

Not many people learn they're adopted as an adult. There's no one to talk to who's been in my shoes. It's a lonely feeling, even though I have Alex around. I'm looking over a fence into a yard filled with those not adopted.

Like Dad, I too have some arrangements to make.

When Alex and I got back to the house, I went into Dad's office and called Rick Montgomery.

"Rick, this is Lance." I said when he answered.

"Lance, I'm so sorry to hear about Devin. Alice called all of us."

"Thanks, Rick. I need some information."

"How can I help?"

"Rick, shortly before Dad died, he used the words 'Christine' and 'adopted.' Aunt Alex told me my background, but she has no clue about Christine. Do you know a Christine, and did you know I was adopted?"

"Yes, I knew you were adopted, but I didn't know you'd never been told. I referred Devin and Erin to an agency in Seattle. My sister was the supervisor for adoptions there at the time."

"Do you know anything about this 'Christine'?"

"I don't know who she is, but she gets half the estate according to your dad's will. You get the Malibu house; she the apartment house in Santa Monica. The Tucson house is split 50/50 when it's sold. I thought that last minute change in your Dad's will was strange. He refused to tell me who Christine was. I could speculate, but that wouldn't be helpful at this time. When I asked Devin who she was, he said, 'Let's just say she's a close relative.'

Wish I could be more helpful to you with that. He left information with me, a manila envelope and a box. I was instructed to give them to you after his death. Perhaps the answers are all there."

"Rick, could you bring all that out tomorrow morning? I need to have it."

"I'll do that, but it'll have to be early."

"That's not a problem. Alex and I probably won't be getting much sleep tonight. Who else knew I was adopted?"

"I'm not sure anyone else knew. Cliff and Billy never knew to my knowledge. Your parents kept it a secret as far as I know."

"How did they do that?"

"Lance, your dad was an actor, and your mother was also an accomplished actress. Both of them were capable of pulling off a ruse. They hated publicity and dreaded any story that might possibly be made by some reporter to appear scandalous."

"Yeah, both were fine actors, and they definitely knew how to avoid publicity."

"Your dad filmed a movie on location in the Seattle area during the spring of 1970. He and Erin had flown to Seattle and applied for adoption in September 1969. In January or February 1970, a young pregnant woman requested help from the agency. My sister felt that your parents were a good match for this young woman's child."

"Do you know her name?"

"Unfortunately, I don't, and my sister moved to another position years ago, so she no longer has access to those records. After your dad's film wrapped in August, he went to the ranch in Redding to be with your mother. They remained secluded. I heard someone say once, that your mother had told them she thought she might be pregnant. Then in early September, they flew to Seattle to get you. They returned to Malibu with you in their arms. 'Our son,' they told everyone."

"And no one ever suspected?"

"Not that I know. I heard someone say once that Erin didn't look pregnant, but that was early on. I never heard that again. They managed to pull it off."

"Why do you think they did all this?"

"As far as I know, they feared Hollywood gossip and you being called 'their adopted son.' They did it to shield you from growing up labeled. Why you weren't told at some point, I don't know. Are you okay?"

"I'm still shaken by Dad's death and this Christine and adoption revelation, but I'm okay. Thanks, Rick. I appreciate your sharing all this."

"You're welcome. If I can be of further help, please call me. I'll bring the information Devin left with me out in the morning. When is Devin's service?"

"Aunt Alex and I haven't talked about that yet. We'll let you know in the next day or two. Thanks, Rick."

After I told Aunt Alex about my conversation with Rick, she said, "Lance, I'm sure the information Rick brings out will be helpful and provide answers to your questions or you will find all the answers when you finish your dad's journals and your mom's diaries."

"I hope so. I know Mom and Dad would never have hurt me. Now I have some investigative work to do, a lot of it."

"Yeah, I think you do. I'll help you if I can. We need to talk about your dad's service."

"I'll call the funeral home and Pastor Sam in the morning, and we can work the service details out then."

Chapter Ten

Erin's Diary, Friday, January 31, 1969

Dev has a busy schedule. It's been that way since he got into film. I've spent my available time working in the church programs, but I've loved every minute of it. I have ample time to support Dev. He hasn't ignored me, having devoted as much time to me as his schedule allows. We have time for at-home candlelight dinners, playing the piano and singing, dancing on the patio in the moonlight, walking along the beach, talking, and taking vacations between films.

I'm grateful that Dev has worked steadily. His earnings have been safely and wisely invested for us by Cliff and Rick. We want for nothing, but live simply. We have a good life, private as we can make it with Dev being in the public eye.

We're only missing one thing—children. We both want them.

Erin's Diary, Wednesday, March 19, 1969

Dev and I think we've improved the media situation. In order to avoid intrusions into our lives by the news media and photographers, we've been making ourselves available for interviews and photo sessions, both in-home and elsewhere, but we've decided when we have children they'll be kept away from all photo sessions because of security concerns. There's always the possibility of kidnapping and ransom demands. That is such a scary thought for us. Our consideration of media needs seems to have led to a peaceful co-existence and a bit more privacy. We've only had a few difficult situations. Neither Dev nor I like being in the news.

Erin's Diary, Monday April 21, 1969

Our dreams of having a family seem to have been buried in Dev's schedule and my volunteer work at church which keeps us both busy. Dev slowly began to notice that at the few parties we attend, even those with our closest friends Billy, Cliff, Rick, and their spouses, I've seemed distracted and aloof. These events have become depressing for me. Last evening about eleven after returning from a party, he noticed I was in some distant place. He asked, "Erin is something troubling you?"

"I'm fine, Dev. Really I am." He noticed tears had welled in my eyes.

"No, you aren't. Did something happen at the party?"

"It's just the same thing that's been happening for the last few years. Only it bothers me more and more."

"What's that?"

"Every time we go to these events, even those with Billy, Cliff, and Rick, the women talk about their children. It's always their children."

"Isn't that normal?"

"It is for them certainly. But I don't have children. I feel they're in some special club, and I'm looking in. I'm an outsider, Dev."

"Do any of them comment about our having no children?"

"Of course not, but I'm left out of the conversation."

"How so?"

I now had tears rolling down my cheeks. Devin moved over to hold me.

"Dev, since they all have children, they have all this information they share. I don't have the information, and I have no way to get it."

"Except with children, right?"

As he held me, my sobbing made it difficult to speak. "Yes, but we don't have any. I always thought children were a part of married life. We've been married almost five years and don't have any. Where are they?"

"I don't have that answer."

"Maybe there's something wrong with me. Mom always had difficulty after I was born. Maybe we need to see Dr. Wray. She'll know what to do."

"She probably will."

"Then if you don't mind, I'll call first thing in the morning and arrange an appointment."

"Do that. Now, let's get to bed. I have to shoot three scenes tomorrow." He kissed me. "Erin, this is going to work out fine. Don't worry about it."

Neither of us slept well that evening, but at least the subject was out in the open. I feel so much better knowing I no longer have to pretend, cry in private, or bear this alone. Dev understands and is supportive.

Devin's Journal, Thursday May 1, 1969

Dr. Wray referred us to a specialist in LA. We endured days of tests. Following the tests, the doctor said to us, "Fortunately, the test results are all within normal limits. Unfortunately, sometimes there are normal couples who have no children or have difficulty conceiving. If you wish a child soon, I'd suggest you adopt. Newborns and small babies are available from many agencies. You'd be amazed at the number of couples who have a biological child following adoption."

Neither of us said a word until we were back in the car.

Erin began sobbing as I held her. Through the sobs, she said, "Why is this happening to me, to us? We can't have children. What did we do?"

"We did nothing, sweetheart. This will all work out. It will. God has a plan for us. We're just not privy to His plans."

"Dev, I just want to be normal. I want to experience that first touch of a newborn. Our friends have kids. Why can't we?"

"I don't know. We'll get through this. You'll see. Boy, talk about shattering dreams. That doctor did it."

"I always dreamed I'd grow up, marry someone wonderful, and... Well, I grew up, and I married you, my Mr. Wonderful. But the rest of the dream was a family. Why is this happening?"

"I wish I knew, Erin. I also always thought I'd have kids, but my thoughts were vague about it all."

"What are we going to do? I just want to be normal."

"There are other ways. Maybe we should adopt and see what happens."

I'm not sure that's going to relieve this pain, this emptiness. We've decided to give ourselves a few months, and then next year talk to someone about adoption if nothing has happened before that. I feel better now we have some sort of idea where we're going.

Erin's Diary, Friday May 2, 1969

Neither of us shared any of this information. We both knew insensitive remarks can be made by the most well-intentioned people. Infertility is painful; any insensitivity from others would only make it more painful.

I have this horrible sense of loss. The pain of being a childless woman seems to permeate my life, but things have been this way for a long time. I feel as if I'm drowning in an ocean of parents, all on lifeboats chattering about their kids. Seeing children anywhere is difficult, a constant reminder. Buying a friend a baby shower gift, watching babies in television commercials, or seeing baby pictures in magazine advertisements are all painful. I just feel this profound sadness.

Both Dev and I wonder what will happen to us in old age or at death. Who will be there to help? Who will care? We both feel this loss and the pain.

Devin's Journal, Saturday, August 2, 1969

About a week ago I said to Erin, "We've waited long enough. I've given a lot of thought to this. I don't have a problem with adoption."

Erin didn't at first find my words comforting, but over the course of the next few days came to the conclusion I was right. She finally concluded, as I had, what she really wants is a baby, regardless of how the baby comes to us. We weren't members of that special parent club to which we wanted entry.

Erin's Diary, Monday, August 4, 1969

Dev and I both know with him being a public figure, his family comes under public scrutiny. We certainly don't want any publicity over an adoption. We've concluded seeking an adoption in California might become public. Neither of us has any desire to be in the public eye any more than we already are, and we certainly don't want attention focused on a child, at least not for being adopted. We've sought Rick's advice. Rick's sister in Seattle, Sally Anne, is a social worker at an adoption agency. She works with clients seeking alternatives to abortion. He'll check with her about possibilities of arranging a private, out-of-state adoption.

Devin's Journal, Monday, August 18, 1969

Rick called me today with the news Sally's agency is willing to do an out-of-state adoption for us. She wanted the two of us to fly up and meet with her."

Erin's Diary, Wednesday, September 10, 1969

Yesterday Dev and I anxiously entered the building housing Center for Hope, a few blocks from Lake Union in Seattle, took the stairs to the second floor, walked down the hall, and entered the reception area for Rick's sister's office. At the receptionist's desk we announced, "We're Devin and Erin Bradshaw. We have an appointment with Sally Anne Ward. Here are the completed forms she asked us to bring to the appointment."

"I'll take these to Sally Anne, and once she reviews them, she'll be out to see you."

About ten minutes later, a distinguished lady in her mid-to-late forties approached us. "Mr. and Mrs. Bradshaw, it's nice to see you. I'm Sally Anne, Ricardo's sister. Well, to be exact, his much older sister." We shook hands.

"Pleased to meet you," said Erin.

"It's nice to meet you, also. So, Rick had a sister I never met?" said Devin. "I don't think we ever met in San Jacinto."

"No, we didn't. Why I'm not sure. Let's go to the office now and get started."

We entered her office, and Sally indicated we take the two chairs facing her desk. "Ricardo tells me the two of you have kept in touch

over the years, Mr. Bradshaw. Would you rather I use your professional name, MacArthur?"

"Yes, Rick and I've kept in touch all these years. And if it wouldn't
violate some professional protocol, please call us, Devin and Erin."

"Then, I'm Sally. Thanks for returning the forms completed.
That'll help us move along quickly."

"I note you refer to him as Ricardo. I've always known him as
Rick."

Sally laughed. "There's a reason for that, sort of a family secret.
Dad insisted I have an Anglo name. So, when Ricardo came along
years later, Mom told him, 'I gave in on the name for the first one.
I'm naming the boy.' Thus, he became Ricardo Martinez Montgomery. He's been Ricardo since within the family, although Dad
often refers to him as Rick. Mom has a fit when he does that."

"That's funny," Devin said, "because when Cliff and I met him in
school, he said, 'Call me Rick. Dad does.'"

Sally laughed. "Mom would have killed him if she'd heard that."
She paused. "I asked you to bring some pictures of yourselves. Did
you?"

I reached into my purse. "We did." I handed them across the
desk.

"Thanks. You indicate on the forms that you would like a
newborn."

"We would." Devin responded.

"You meet all our requirements for adoptive parents. Your income far exceeds our minimum." She looked at us and smiled. "Ricardo has highly recommended you. I note you have been married over five years. Have there been any pregnancies?"

"None, I'm sorry to say. The doctor has suggested adoption," said Erin.

"Do you want a male or female infant, Devin?"

"Either."

"Erin, do you agree?"

"I do."

"Yeah, I know the two of you just want a baby." She smiled again at us. "Erin, do you intend to continue your church work after we've placed a baby in your home?"

"No, I'll be leaving my position at the end of the year, so by January I'll be home full-time."

"Great. I like to hear that from clients, but unfortunately not all couples have that luxury. Now, I must tell you both how I select adoptive parents. I am a stickler for matching—nationality backgrounds, height, eye and hair color, age, and educational backgrounds. That's the reason for the pictures and some of the questions on our forms."

Dev said, "But we don't..."

"Yes, I know, Devin. You and Erin just want a baby, but I think this is important. First, I want the child to look like he or she belongs with the parents, and second, in your case, you're a public figure. Ricardo said you wanted privacy, and that you didn't want or need gossip columnists asking questions. Your child doesn't need that either. Growing up is difficult enough for children without some publicity hound always poking around. So I want my placement in your home to look as much like your biological child as I can. Okay?"

Both of us responded, "Yes." No point in stating we didn't care about all the matching. However, we saw her reasoning, especially as it applied to our situation.

"Now, let me turn to the bad news." We both felt the unexpected hit. "You may have a long wait, perhaps two years. You both have college degrees. I want one or both birth parents to have earned college degrees. That creates its own difficulty. If there are no college backgrounds, I want one or both parents having excellent high school records so there is the potential to earn a college degree. Are there any questions?"

We both had thought: Is all this necessary just because we have college degrees? All we want is a baby.

"Yes, we have one question," I said, "both Dev and I would like assurance that neither parent has a past with drug usage. Is that possible?"

"That may be difficult. We may not be able to interview both birth parents to obtain that assurance, and sometimes we're not given accurate information anyway. But I promise you, I'll do my best to find out."

"Thanks, Sally," said Dev.

"I want both of you to go home, relax, and think about a nursery. I'll call you as soon as I have good news. Hopefully, that'll be sooner than we anticipate."

Sally escorted us out of the office and into the hall where we said our goodbyes.

Erin's Diary, Saturday, December 27, 1969

We've still had no word from the adoption agency. These last few months have been difficult for us. We spent a few days at our ranch in Redding.

We purchased furniture and decorated one of the Malibu bedrooms as a nursery. I dropped hints to Mona about wanting a baby soon and similar hints to our friends.

We're looking forward to 1970 and a baby.

Erin's Diary, Thursday, January 29, 1970

It's been a wonderful day. This afternoon the phone rang.

Sally Anne called to tell us a new client came in a few days ago, pregnant. She wants to place her baby for adoption. She has an associate degree from a community college; the father has a university degree. Everything seems to match well. She was assured there's been no drug use and thinks this will be the child for us, a baby due in September.

A plan is already developing in my mind as to how this baby scenario will unfold over the coming months. Dev and I, when he's finished filming on location in the Seattle area during the spring, would remain secluded at the Redding ranch until September. Then we'll fly to Seattle when the time comes, and fly back to LA with our little surprise. I'm sure Dev will go along with my plan.

Erin's Diary, Saturday, January, 31, 1970

I've had a busy yesterday and today. We've bought some newborn items and clothing, at least that which could be purchased not knowing our child's sex. The nursery is a big hint to Mona, but I've been on the phone and dropped even more baby news to some strategic friends. We flew to Sacramento yesterday. Tim, our ranch hand, picked us up and drove us to Redding and the ranch.

Erin's Diary, Tuesday, September 8, 1970

We're in Renton, just south of Seattle, and now have a son. These last four days have been busy ones. He's sleeping now, our little Lance Evan Bradshaw.

Tuesday evening, the 4th, was a long one for us. The next morning, September 5, at 8:21 a.m., our little boy was born.

He's a healthy, beautiful, blue-eyed blond, perfect in every way we think, with long fingers and long legs. Of course, we counted his fingers and toes. None were missing.

One of the nurses on duty said the first time she handed him to us, "Congratulations. Not only is he a perfect specimen, he's beautiful. Enjoy him."

Little Lance stretched and opened his eyes. With that movement, a place for him was carved in our hearts, a movement like none we'd ever seen. He reached out his little hand, and I touched his palm with my index finger. The little hand closed around my finger sending a warm current surging through my body, instantaneous, piercing, endearing; this was the newborn warmth I'd sometimes thought I'd never experience. Dev was equally shaken the first time he held our little Lance.

I've noticed he seems to react to us as though we are strangers. Odd. Is there fear in that little face? Newborns can't remember their birth mothers or can they?

Erin's Diary, Friday, September 11, 1970

Lance is sleeping now in our nursery. Yesterday, September 10th, our son was released from the hospital to us.

Sally Anne gave us a document identifying Lance as our child. It is the only official document we'll have until the adoption is finalized in a year, she'd said.

September 10, 1975

To Whom It May Concern:

This is to verify that Lance Evan Bradshaw, born on September 5, 1970, is in the home of Mr. and Mrs. Devin Bradshaw, 2101 Winding Pacific Trail, Malibu, California, having been placed there by a Washington State Court Order for the purpose of adoption. The parents have total responsibility for said child. They have no birth certificate because it is not issued until the Final Adoption Order is made in approximately one year. As the responsible agency which placed the child, we are submitting this letter as proof of the family's responsibility for the health and welfare of the child.

Sally Anne Ward,
Supervisor of Adoptions

Center for Hope

Seattle, Washington

Devin had arranged a private plane to fly us back to LAX to avoid any media attention. I'm so glad we had that privacy.

Erin's Diary, Monday, September 14, 1970

This morning, a short statement was released to the press by Rick and Cliff: "Devin and Erin MacArthur are pleased to announce the birth of their first child. At this time, they have not named the child."

We aren't releasing additional statements. I hope this meets media needs. We don't want attention, especially on the baby.

Chapter Eleven

Thursday, June 11, 1992, Morning

Early this morning Rick brought out the manila envelope and box Dad had left with him.

I took them into the study, placed them on the desk, sat in Dad's chair, leaned back, and closed my eyes. Did I really want to open them? Was there more upsetting information inside? I just looked at the box as my emotions churned.

Having experienced my mother's death didn't make my father's any easier. Does one death ever make another easier? I needed more time with him. I was angry with myself for not coming home to spend time with him during his final days. Being the obedient person I am has its disadvantages, but I'd never been rebellious.

I suppose letting go of one you love is always difficult. Parents are supposed to die in old age, aren't they? Losing both parents was devastating. It had always been the three of us. I was now alone, except for Aunt Alex, plus I had another family and background that caused me concern. Then there was this Christine. She had to be a sister. A step-sister, I guess. I had to find her.

I'm not sure how long I stayed there. Finally, I rose and headed for the kitchen, some coffee, and a bite to eat. Alex was waiting for me. She'd prepared breakfast. Aunt Alex and I ate quietly and put our dishes in the dishwasher.

We brought our coffee into the study and sat down, she on the sofa and I at the desk. I opened the manila envelope. There were three letters inside from Dad, two in envelopes with my name on them. One was marked "Christine." I wouldn't open that one. The envelopes with my name were dated April 19, 1992, and April 29, 1992. I opened the one written earlier and began reading aloud:

April 19, 1992

Dear Lance,

Since you are now reading this, I hope we had time to talk after your graduation. If not, this letter will explain things your mother and I should have told you long ago.

I hope you know how much your mother and I loved you. We have always been grateful for all the joy you brought into our lives. I thank you.

What I must tell you now is something I hope I shared with you; if not, I'm so sorry. For many reasons we thought it best not to tell you, but I realized too late it was wrong of us not to have done so. I pray you can find it in your heart to forgive us.

What we should've told you when you were very young is that you were adopted...

I paused and looked up at Alexa. She smiled sadly and said, "Well, he did try to tell you personally rather than in a letter, but..."

"He didn't have the time. I should've come home after he flew to Tucson."

"Lance, you know that would have only upset him at a time when he didn't need being upset."

"Maybe, but we'd have had time together. Time we needed. Time I wanted."

"Your dad thought you would have that time."

"Well, we didn't. I'd have liked to have asked him some questions about my adoption."

"I know you would have, but this is simply a bump on the road called life. When your Dad's world turned upside down, he continued on. His good humor remained intact. Lance, I know you have questions and need answers. Your dad's journals and mom's diaries might provide answers."

"When I finish reading them."

"You were their son in every respect except one, the least important one."

"I know I was. Maybe it's just a bump in the road, but it feels more like a mountain to climb at the moment."

We were silent for a moment before I slowly began to read again.

> ...adopted through an agency in Seattle, Center for Hope, a private agency supported by many Seattle area churches. Rick Montgomery's sister was the director at the time, but she's no longer there. You'll find the agency contact information in the box, along with some information on your biological family.
>
> Your mother and I never had any other information on your biological family except what the agency provided us at the time of your adoption.
>
> As your Aunt Alex is now your only remaining family member except for Christine, you might at some point in the future want to search for your biological family. I think Alex will be able and

willing to stick around and assist you in any search.
Alex was always my support growing up; she will
be there for you now. I'm sure your girlfriend Alle
will also be supportive. By the way, if I didn't say it
before now, I liked Alle. She seemed a good match.
You might want to hang onto her.

I looked up and smiled at Alexa, who was also smiling, and
said, "Alle's a keeper." Then I returned to reading.

Knowing now you're adopted, you'll probably have
questions about your biological family. Answers to
these questions may prove beneficial. I recommend
you make the search when you feel ready, now or
sometime in the future. It seems to me that you
might prefer to know something about them before
you have children of your own.

I've included everything we had; I think it will help
you in any search. There are also some other items
that I didn't want misplaced, our wedding rings
for instance. Billy, Cliff, and Rick will provide any
further help you may need and/or answer questions
you may have about the estate.

Always remember your mom and I loved you.

All my Love,

Dad

I put the letter aside and began reading the second letter:

April 29, 1992

Dear Lance,

I know this may come as a bigger shock than your being adopted, but I have to share it with you and ask that you grant me one last wish. Please find Christine for me and pass along my letter to her. She must have my letter; she may need it! Leaving you and her is easier for me knowing you will find her.

You wonder who Christine is no doubt. When you go through the photo albums, you will see a few pictures of her at ages five and ten.

I'll briefly explain Christine and her mother, Anna. I told your mom about Anna when I asked her to marry me; she understood. She was always supportive of me and any relationship I was permitted to have with Christine.

When you read my journals and your mom's diaries, you will rediscover your parents, wrinkles and all, on our journey through this life. There is much we never shared with you I regret to say.

I met Anna when I was a sophomore, the first of September (1958), at the U of A. Her full name was Anna Christine Taylor. She was a New Yorker whose grandparents wintered in Tucson, thus her enrollment at the U of A. She was intelligent, interesting, pretty, and blonde. I liked her. We dated each other exclusively from the end of October until just before Christmas break when I broke off the relationship. My thoughts at the time are recorded in one of the journals, I'm sure. She was my second rather serious relationship; the first having ended because I wanted an acting career. At the time, I was always more interested in a long-term career in acting than in any relationship, serious or not. That is until I met your mother. Erin was the love of my life from the beginning. I hope that's true for you and Alle.

Anna, I think, was looking for a long-term permanent relationship with me from the beginning, but I have no firm reason as to why I thought that, then or now. In any case, there was one evening in early December (1958) when we became intimate. No, I didn't have too much alcohol to use as an excuse. I was simply overcome with passion and didn't engage my brain. That's how I viewed it then and now.

In March 1959, Anna abruptly left the U of A and returned to her home in New York. She did leave me a note with something in it about my leaving her a "wonderful gift." That gift turned out to be Christine. She said she would eventually contact me, and she did. Twice, in fact! Both times at ages when Christine would probably not have connected her father with the film star.

There are many things I've always wanted to tell Christine. But at ages five and ten I thought saying those things age inappropriate. Your mother agreed. Hugs and kisses are wonderful, but they're never enough. Fathers and daughters, like fathers and sons, should share lives. They should be more than passing strangers in the night as was the case between your grandfather and me.

I never saw Christine after our visit with her at age ten. I did make the effort to locate her through the years, but was never successful.

Please, grant me one last wish. Find her! Give her my letter! If she is willing to listen, tell her about me, let her read our journals, and provide any help she may need.

You will find the return address on the two letters I received from Anna when Christine turned five and ten. Those letters are inside two of the journals. They may help in locating them. I suggest using the private detective I have used for years to track them. He was never successful in locating them, but now seems to have a lead. Gerry's contact information is in my desk as are his two letters to me. Maybe you will get a break.

Thanks for being the son and loving person you always were.

Son, I love you,

Dad

As I put Dad's letters aside, I looked at Alex and said, "Now I know for certain about Christine. I still wish they'd told me in person long ago about the two of us."

"I understand, Lance. I wish they'd told you long ago also."

"You know Aunt Alex, I wonder how I'd have felt and reacted at age nine or ten had I been told about Christine and my adoption."

"I'm not sure, but I doubt the information would have been such a blow, Lance."

"Well, I wish it'd happened like that."

"Unfortunately, it didn't. I'm sorry."

We were silent for a moment before I opened the box. The first items I found in the box were three birth certificates, Dad's, Mom's, and mine. After examining the three, I handed them to Aunt Alex, saying, "I've never examined my birth certificate before. Why doesn't mine list my biological parents' names?"

After examining the three certificates briefly, she said, "They're from different states, but I'm not certain. Yours is probably what's called an amended birth certificate. A friend with an adopted child told me once that states now issue an amended birth certificate to an adoptee in order to keep the names of the birth parents secret. Maybe you can ask Rick about it."

"I will, but guess that could explain it."

Looking inside the box again, I found Mom's death certificate, then Mom and Dad's marriage license. Under the license was a ring box. Opening it, I found Dad's wedding band and that beautiful ring Mom always wore, the wedding ring Dad had given her, a ring they loved. Copies of both Mom's and Dad's wills were next with a paper-clipped note for me to see Rick soon about Dad's will. As I glanced over Dad's will and the codicil I noted the division of property between Christine and me. Then I found deeds to all of Dad's property with a post-it note to see Cliff about the pending sale of the ranch outside Redding. Included also were bond, stock, certificates of deposit, and all the banking information. The last item in the box was a document from Center for Hope in Seattle, my adoption record!

Center for Hope
Seattle, Washington

NON-IDENTIFYING INFORMATION FROM ADOPTION RECORD OF:

LANCE EVAN BRADSHAW

ADOPTIVE CHILD/ADULT ADOPTEE HISTORY: Lance was born on September 5, 1970, in King County, Washington. The pregnancy was full term. After approximately twenty (20) hours of labor, Lance was delivered vaginally. His birth weight was seven (7) pounds, eight (8) ounces, and his height was twenty-two (22) inches. His discharge weight from the hospital was seven (7) pounds, five (5) ounces, and he was described as a normal infant. He joined his adoptive family on 9-5-70.

MATERNAL HISTORY: Lance's birth mother was twenty-one (21) years old when Lance was born. She was a very attractive young lady, 5'6" tall, weighing 110 pounds, with blue eyes, a fair complexion, and blonde hair. She was of English and Swedish descent. She was a community college graduate and had been an excellent student, both in high school and college. She was employed as an executive secretary at the time of Lance's birth. She reported she enjoyed tennis and liked to read. She began pre-natal care during her first month of pregnancy and there were no complications throughout her pregnancy. She had not taken medication of any kind during her pregnancy, and her health was very good. Lance's birth mother had no siblings.

She made the decision to place her child for adoption because she did not feel either financially or emotionally prepared to assume the responsibility of parenting. She was no longer involved with Lance's birth father at the time of Lance's birth and desired that her son have a two-parent family with a stable, loving marriage.

PATERNAL HISTORY: Lance's birth father was twenty-six (26) years old when Lance was born and was married. He was 6'3" tall, had an athletic build, brown hair and eyes, and a dark complexion. He was of French and Italian decent. He liked tennis, golf, and reading. His personality was described as being outgoing and friendly. He had a college degree in aeronautical engineering and was employed as an engineer. Though his relationship with Lance's birth mother was discontinued at the time of Lance's birth, he was aware of her adoption plan. Lance's birth mother also reported that his birth father didn't provide her any financial support throughout her pregnancy, but neither did her parents. Lance's birth father had three siblings.

Prepared by:

Sally Anne Ward

Supervisor of Adoptions

I handed the document to Aunt Alex when I finished reading. I was overwhelmed with this information on my birth family, my other family. My birth father seemed to take no responsibility for his actions, unlike the father I'd always known. My birth mother seemed a responsible person, someone I could admire in many respects. She, I thought, I might want to meet.

My thoughts were perplexing as Alex finished reading the document and said, "Lance, what do you think?"

"I'm not sure what to think. This is a family I never knew I had. I think I'd like to contact my birth mother, but I'm not sure I even want to meet my birth father. Also, I have to locate Christine, not just for Dad, but for me also. After this day, I'm simply emotionally exhausted and need to walk to clear my head. Do you mind if I go down to the beach?"

"Not at all. Later we can discuss this in more detail if you wish. The road ahead may be clearer after a night's rest. I'll stay here for a few minutes."

When Dad died, I thought my last link to my past had died also. Now, I know that's not true. I have another past. One I'm going to have to uncover.

I know Dad spent days wondering each evening if he'd see tomorrow. I think I'll see tomorrow. Hopefully, many of them, but… would those tomorrows be happy ones?

Chapter Twelve

June 1992

The days before Dad's funeral were not easy for either Aunt Alex or me. We spent our time getting to know one another better, looking through photo albums, and reading many of Dad's journals and Mom's diary entries. Getting acquainted was a welcome diversion for me. Perhaps that was the major reason Dad asked her to stay with me and be here after his death.

Two days after Dad's death as we were going through some of Dad's photo albums, I noticed photos I couldn't recall having seen before. They were of a child and Dad. One was with Mom. I asked Aunt Alex, "Do you think that's Christine with Dad and Mom in these pictures?"

"I assume it is. Is there anything written on the back?"

I carefully removed a few of the pictures, turned them over, and there in Mom's handwriting were the words, "Dev and Christine in Central Park" or "Christine with me." No dates appeared on the back of any of the pictures.

"Well, Lance, you have pictures from long ago and a location, but you still have no clue where she is now."

"I'm going to find out."

"I'm sure you will. These pictures remind me that Devin and I had a wonderful childhood. We were always close friends as kids. Dad was always busy and aloof, but Mom was the backbone of the family. She was the weld that held us together with her love and warmth. Your grandmother was a tolerant lady and taught us tolerance, but your grandmother could be one tough, yet fair lady, Lance."

"I wish I remembered her."

"I wish you did too."

"What did you study at OU?"

"I majored in business, with lots of accounting and finance courses. By profession, I was a banker. That's how I met your uncle David."

"What was Uncle Dave like?"

"He was tall, attractive, but not movie star handsome like Devin, more rugged, outdoorsy handsome. He had a great sense of humor, laughed a lot, and loved life. You would have liked David Riley."

"How did you meet him?"

"He always joked that I trapped him, but I didn't. He had inherited his father's oil business. His family had always used the bank where I worked. He came into the bank one day asking for advice on investing money--a lot of it--he had received from the sale of some property he'd inherited from his parents. Obviously, he was satisfied with my advice because we began dating and later married. He was a wonderful husband and companion."

"So he had oil money?"

"Yes, but he also had lots of property. I wouldn't call him or us super wealthy, but some might have. In any case, we had a little money and lived "high on the hog" as some would say in Oklahoma. We lived in Dave's parents' home in Nichols Hills."

"A nice area?"

"Well, it's not Malibu or Hollywood. It's an older section of Oklahoma City and has lovely homes."

"Lance, I was so happy when you came along. You were a nephew I could see, hold, and hug. Now I also have a niece out there somewhere."

"I recall a bit about Uncle Dave's funeral."

"I'm so glad all of you came. Dave fell from an oil rig. I always wondered what he was doing up on that thing in the first place. He ordinarily didn't do things like that. Even his co-workers had no explanation."

"That must have been really tough for you."

"It was. Still is in many ways. I understand what you're experiencing. At least, I understand in part. Now, I want to hear more about you."

"Mom and Dad were a bit overprotective. Why, I'm not sure. Could have been because I was adopted? The overprotection was never a serious problem for me; I was the easy-going, compliant type anyway, but I always felt something or someone was missing. And for some reason, I always feared being rejected. My friends seemed to feel my overprotective parents a problem, but I was aware of what was happening in their homes; thus, I always felt secure in my parents' overprotectiveness. That was especially true as I became older and more aware."

"You turned out just fine. Where'd you go to school?"

"Except for kindergarten, I was sent to Catholic elementary and high schools. No doubt to prevent as much unapproved influence on me as possible considering the Hollywood influences surrounding me. I always enjoyed those schools, had wonderful teachers and great friends."

"Were you involved in sports?"

"I was a swimmer when I was younger, but didn't like the competitive aspects so gave it up. I only swim for fun now. I was active in theatre. Unlike Dad, I preferred backstage work. I was

always intrigued watching play directors and Dad's film directors perform their duties. Thus, I grew up wanting to direct and
tended toward wanting to teach theatre."

"At the high school level?"

"No, I'd prefer college. My degree from Arizona is in educational theatre. In order to teach college, I have to return to Arizona for a master's in theatre, like Dad. Only, I won't emphasize
acting as he did. Instead, I'll emphasize lighting, scene design,
costuming, makeup, and directing, the technical side. Dad never seemed unhappy the times we discussed this. He and mom
always wanted me to sail my own ship."

"You're a young man who knows where he's headed. I like
that. What about sports in high school?"

"I played a little tennis, but I was better in track. Go into my
room upstairs. There are a few trophies. Mom never missed a
meet, and Dad was able to attend many of them."

"Lance, when your dad and I grew up, Thanksgiving and
Christmas were the holidays we looked forward to. Was it the
same with you?"

"Yes, but New Year's was a special time. Why Mom and Dad
began the tradition, I never knew, but those times together and
the memories are cherished. The tradition began when I was very
young. I was always included in Mom and Dad's New Year's Eve
celebration whether at our house or the home of close friends.
We played cards and board games, but for me as a youngster it
was also a time to enjoy all those forbidden snacks and stay up
late. As I became older, I loved being able to stay up and see a
New Year roll in."

"I'll bet you did."

"The tradition continued until I graduated from high school,
a tradition I plan to continue when I have a family. The New
Year's Eve celebrations after Mom's death were always spent

alone with Dad at some LA night spot. Dad and I were just two lonely individuals tossing about in a turbulent sea of New Year's Eve revelers. Not much fun, but Dad was lonely. So off we went for those lonely evenings together. As midnight approached, the celebrating around us intensified, yet we were sadly reminiscing happy times in our past."

"I can imagine."

"I had an easy life and a good one most people would say. It was easy until Mom was killed. I've not forgotten much of the day."

*****

Both Dad and Mona were in the ER waiting room when I rushed in. "Dad, how's Mom?" I asked.

"We don't know anything yet," he answered.

"What happened?"

"An accident is all the policeman told me. I'm not sure he even knew."

"How serious is she?"

"Lance, we just don't know," Mona responded. "We're waiting for someone to tell us."

Every person entering the room had our immediate attention. Even as we paced the room, we noticed those entering. None were doctors or nurses.

We sat. Mona prayed, tears in her eyes. Dad and I were also praying, his arm around me.

Soon we noticed a nurse approaching us. We rose. "Mr. Bradshaw?" she asked.

"Yes. How's my wife?"

"I'll take you back now. The doctor will see you shortly."

We followed. She finally escorted us through the surgical ward door. A few feet down the hall, we were told to wait in a small, windowless, carpeted room, a claustrophobic enclosure. In the corner was a small table holding a lamp and a box of Kleenex. Kleenex? Not a good sign. On one side of the table was a small sofa, on the other, an arm chair. Mona and I sat on the sofa, her arm draped around my shoulder. Dad stood, fidgeting, leaning against the wall.

The door opened and a doctor entered. "Mr. Bradshaw? I'm Dr. Fowler."

"Yes. How's my wife?"

"I'm sorry. We did everything possible. She never regained consciousness."

"She'll be okay, won't she?"

"I'm sorry, but your wife didn't survive." I began crying as Mona held me.

"Of course, she did. There must be some mistake."

"Her injuries were too severe. I'm sorry."

"What do you mean? What kind of injuries?"

"A head injury and internal bleeding."

"Noooo…not Erin," he half screamed as he slid down the wall onto the floor and cried. All of us were now sobbing.

"What…will I do without her? How can we…?" Dad looked at the doctor, opened his mouth to continue, but Mona interrupted.

"We understand, Doctor. Don't we, Devin?"

Dad whispered a painful, "Yes."

I felt empty, inert, and sick to my stomach. I understood all too well.

The doctor stood quietly, patiently, then gently asked, "Would you like to see her now?"

Dad and I nodded yes. We began to follow him.

We followed the doctor into the hall, a tunnel, dark and foreboding, towards the room where Mom had been left.

When we reached the door, the doctor stood aside as we tentatively entered the dimly lit room. I noticed a cut on Mom's forehead, lacerations on her right cheek and on both arms as we neared the bed, but otherwise Mom just appeared to be sleeping. Dad sat beside the bed and took her hand, lifeless, yet still warm. Sobs and tears began. "Erin, I'm here now." She didn't respond. "What am I to do?" Again, there was no response. Slowly, it must have finally registered that she'd never respond to him again. He leaned over the bed, drawing her into an embrace. "I love you," he cried out. Sobs consumed him.

I stood crying near him. A few minutes later, I touched Dad's shoulder and said, "Dad, would you like to leave now?"

"No," he responded, but Dad knew he must. After kissing Mom, he whispered again, "I love you." He turned, took my arm, and walked me toward the door. At the door, he turned back and said, half to himself, "I didn't say 'I love you' this morning when you left. I hope you knew I did."

I just couldn't leave. I moved back to Mom's side, and touched her hand. I looked at her, then leaned down and kissed her cheek. I straightened. "I'm sorry, Mom. I didn't say I love you this morning either when you left." I looked again at her and moved to join Dad at the door. I still felt sick, just wanting to curl up in a ball, all alone, but Dad needed me. I needed to be strong for him. Moments later, we closed the door, leaving Mom and a major part of our lives behind. It was difficult. Perhaps Dad and I were just trying to be strong for each other.

We walked down the hallway, even longer and darker now, our arms around each other, and into the waiting area. It was the most difficult and longest walk of our lives. A walk we took unwillingly into the unknown, a life without Mom.

*****

"I'd just graduated from high school, Aunt Alex. The weeks since had been happy ones until Mom's accident. I was preparing to enter the university at summer's end, but now it was to be a life without Mom. I always thought parents were supposed to die in their old age."

"We always think that, Lance."

"Somewhere beyond this earthly hell, there's a place called Heaven, a place of peace and serenity, eternity. It's the morning after darkness and shadows, a place which doesn't turn upside down, a land outside darkness. Mom's in that beautiful and peaceful place enjoying the light. Knowing where she is provides joy."

"Yes, Lance, but God surrounds us with love and comfort, even in our worst times also, and so do our friends and relatives."

"Yes, He does. Then, Aunt Alex, about three weeks after Mom's funeral, Dad suddenly announced one morning that we were flying to Honolulu. And after two weeks on beautiful Oahu, we returned feeling better. However, our sorrow in losing Mom always lingered. I'm not certain Dad ever fully recovered. A part of both of us was missing. For Dad, the missing hole was perhaps more severe than mine. He always said Mom was the love of his life. The trip and preparing to enter the university and beginning a new life proved welcome diversions for me. That trip with Dad was a bit strange."

"Strange in what way, Lance?"

"Dad took me to every spot on Oahu he and Mom had visited on their honeymoon. His explanation at each spot seemed to bring him joy, the only joy I'd seen in him since Mom died. Our last stop was at the Blowhole and Honola Cove Beach Lookout. After watching the waves drive the ocean through the Blowhole a few times, he turned, took my arm, and walked me to the right, across the parking lot. At the railing, he simply looked down on Honola Cove Beach, the small beach where the Lancaster/Kerr late-night beach scene in From Here to Eternity had been filmed. I'd been told about the beach many times on visits to Oahu. Looking at him, I could see sorrow, and before long, tears formed in his eyes and slowly began to run down his cheeks. His memories must have been intense and profound. He never said a word, but after a few minutes, he turned, took my arm, and we walked toward our rental. As I followed, I wondered about those memories, memories of Mom no doubt, but said nothing. I had often wondered about those memories until I read Dad's journals and Mom's diaries."

"That spot had special memories for him if you recall what was said in your mom's diaries and dad's journals." I nodded, and she paused briefly looking into the distance as she wiped her eyes, then said, "Lance, do you have a girlfriend?"

"Yeah, her name is Alle."

"Suppose I'll meet her at your dad's service?"

"Yes, you will. I've called her, and she and her parents plan to be there. She reminds me of Mom."

"Did you ever tell her she reminded you of your mom?"

"Yeah, I did. Not the smartest move I ever made, I guess. She looked at me and said 'Lance, are you looking for a mother?' I was stunned. I replied, 'No, Alle, I'm not. I had a mother until I was almost 18. I'm not looking for one in you. There are just certain things about you that remind me of Mom. Is that so bad?'"

"What did she say to that?"

"She said, 'I suppose not, but…'"

I interrupted her and said, "Alle, do I in any way remind you of your father?"

She had a funny little smile and said, "Well, yes. You do."

I jumped at that and told her, "There you see. I'm not a psychological mess." The matter never came up again.

"I suppose had Alle known my father was Devin MacArthur early on in our relationship she might have walked. By the time I told her about my family, she knew me well enough it mattered little. When Dad flew out to Tucson, she came with me to the airport."

"Later, she said, 'It was fascinating to discover I liked the man on a personal level much more than I liked the actor I've seen so many times on the screen.' That was Dad, as charismatic in person as he was on the screen, maybe more so in person."

"I know he was, Lance. I grew up with him. We'll both miss him."

"I already do. More than you'll ever know."

Chapter Thirteen

Devin's Journal, Thursday, July 14, 1988

Erin was not supposed to die at the young age of 47, but she did. My life ended or seemed to end at that moment. I think my tears could have created an ocean, my anguish a tsunami. Will there be better days? I'm not sure; I'm just coping.

I'm still numb. Each day is a new struggle, just putting one foot in front of the other. Her rose garden, pictures in the house, our son, they are all reminders of my loss.

My tears may not be flowing as often, the racking sobs are fewer, but the vivid memories of her never leave me. She was my life for so long. Does saying goodbye ever end? Memories, while pleasant, are a constant reminder of my loss. I long for Erin.

My religion is some comfort, but I still suffer. Does suffering have a purpose? If so, I wish I understood what that was in my case. Perhaps I will eventually understand.

Lance is suffering too, but I'm not much help I fear. I try. I'm sure his faith is of some comfort to him also, but Mona and Ginny have provided much of his comfort, the personal comfort I'm unable to provide as I try to exist in my own sorrow.

How do I go on without Erin? She was at my side for so many years. I miss her smile, her kind words, her touch, her kisses, but most of all I feel my major earthly support is gone. I do have Lance, but it's not the same.

It's been about a week since Officer Pena arrived at the front door to say there'd been an accident, and Erin had been rushed to Mt. Sinai Hospital in LA.

My life went into free-fall at that moment. Thoughts were a jumble. Why had I let her drive into LA alone knowing Lance couldn't go with her? Why had that truck run a red light or so it was thought? Why was no one in the truck when the police arrived? What few leads the police have all reached a dead end. Why? Why couldn't the doctors have saved her? Why? Why? Why? No answers, just questions. I don't think I said "I love you" before she left the house. Did she know how much I loved her? That haunts me. We take life for granted. We need to remember each parting may be the last. Is that too difficult? It was for me it seems. That hurts.

My happy memories of her fade when images of her lying in that hospital bed flash through my mind. She was sleeping. No, she wasn't! Watching her casket lowered into the earth was like watching a star fall, her bright light descending into some darkness, just as my own light descended.

Will I ever stop hurting? I need a change. I must get out of this house and away from these flooding memories for a while.

I think my life really began with Erin. Will it end there?

Chapter Fourteen

Saturday, June 20, 1992

Rick and I released Dad's obituary to the media two days after his death. We listed his survivors as follows:

Mr. MacArthur's survivors are son Lance; daughter Christine; sister Alexa; close friends, Mona Washington, Ginny Washington Thompson, and life-long friends, Cliff and Ann Dunne, Rick and Sue Montgomery, and Billy and Sarah Feldmann.

Yes, that created a bit of media buzz lasting a day or two. Dad's daughter was an unknown fact. Since we provided no further information, the media had a small tidbit which went nowhere for them. Our thinking had been that without the ability to sensationally expand on a known fact public attention would quickly wane.

By the time of Dad's service days later public media speculation had pretty much ceased, but no doubt there was still speculation and investigation occurring in the major Hollywood news media back rooms. The possibility of an unknown scandal was too much for these types to simply ignore.

Rather than calling the funeral home and our pastor about Dad's funeral, I visited each regarding the plans he had made with them. I was so glad that Dad had planned his service in detail. Alex and I were spared that ordeal. We had enough to do and think about other than planning a funeral service. Dad was correct I thought when he'd referred to Mr. White in one of his journals as the funeral home's little, pasty man whose honey dripped. Mr. White bothered me also, or I was simply stressed out. Pastor Sam was helpful and offered comfort, just as he had done four years ago. I was really pleased he agreed to my speaking at Dad's service. He did object to the closing musical number Dad had requested, but he relented, just as he had relented when Dad used the same number for Mom's funeral.

We held Dad's funeral on a beautiful and sunny Santa Monica morning over a week after his death. Saturday had seemed to me a better day for many of his colleagues to attend. Our church in Santa Monica was filled. Unfortunately, I gave no prior thought to fans and media creating a circus-like atmosphere outside, but that was the scene we encountered. Thank goodness, Pastor Sam had alerted the police about possible crowds. Barricades had been erected keeping the curious at bay.

Shortly before the service began, Alex and I took our seats in the front row, close to Dad's casket, covered in roses, much like those from Mom's beloved rose garden. I had asked Alle to sit with us, but she and her parents felt it more appropriate to sit in the row behind.

The service began with the choir and congregation singing "Amazing Grace."

Following "Amazing Grace," Rick rose, walked to the lectern, and read the opening Scripture Dad had requested, Ecclesiastes 3:1-8: *For everything there is a season, and a time for every matter under heaven: a time to be born, and a time to die; a time to plant, and a time to pluck up what is planted; a time to kill, and a time to heal; a time to break down, and a time to build up; a time to weep, and a time to laugh; a time to mourn, and a time to dance; a time to cast away stones, and a time to gather stones together; a time to embrace, and a time to refrain from embracing; a time to seek, and a time to lose; a time to keep, and a time to cast away; a time to tear, and a time to sew; a time to keep silence, and a time to speak; a time to love, and a time to hate; a time for war, and a time for peace.*

Another of Mom and Dad's favorite hymns, "Great is Thy Faithfulness," followed.

Then, Billy read Psalm 23: *The Lord is my shepherd; I shall not want. He makes me lie down in green pastures. He leads me beside still waters. He restores my soul. He leads me in paths of righteousness for his name's sake. Even though I walk through the valley of the shadow of death, I will fear no evil, for you are with me; your rod and your staff, they comfort me. You prepare a table before me in the presence of my enemies; you anoint my head with oil; my cup overflows. Surely goodness and mercy shall follow me all the days of my life, and I shall dwell in the house of the Lord forever.*

The church soloist who often performed at Sunday services began singing "On Eagles Wings."

At the close of the hymn, Cliff, the last of Dad's closest friends, rose, walked to the lectern, and read the final Scripture, Romans 14:7-9: *For none of us lives to himself, and none of us dies to himself. For if we live, we live to the Lord, and if we die, we die to the Lord. So then, whether we live or whether we die, we are the Lord's. For to this end Christ died and lived again, that he might be Lord both of the dead and of the living.*

Pastor Sam MacDonald was already at the pulpit as Cliff returned to his seat. He looked out, smiled sadly, and said, *"Please join me in prayer. Heavenly Father, it is with heavy hearts we come before you, but we rejoice knowing Devin is enjoying your company. We are gathered to celebrate the life of our loved one and friend, and in this time of need, may your comfort be with all of us, but especially Devin's family and friends. We ask these things in the name of Jesus. Amen."*

Pastor Sam continued:

> *I feel a part of Devin's family. I grieve with all of you. Devin had a way of making those he knew feel like friends and family. He was my friend, a friend of many decades.*
>
> *About a year or so after Devin and I met, we had a discussion about a novel he had recently read. He even gave me a copy. It was one of his favorite novels he told me. That novel was Anton*

Myrer's _Once an Eagle_. The novel's main character believed one should live his life as a good man. I know there are various definitions of "a good man," but I've always thought a "good man" was one who not only loved God but also loved others as imperfect as he might be. Devin spent his days on earth as a good man.

I know we may disagree on the definition of the term "a good man." However, there are some men whose life exemplifies for most individuals what "a good man" means.

Most of you present knew him as Devin MacArthur. I, and his family, knew him as Devin or Dad, or Dev as Erin always called him. Devin was more than just a popular film actor. He was also a Christian, a husband, a father, a brother, and a friend to many of you.

I first met Devin, and also Erin, when they began to attend church here soon after moving to Santa Monica in about 1966, over twenty-five years ago. I was then the new pastor in this church.

I've had many conversations with Devin over the years, so I think I knew him well. I also think I knew his heart.

I have been in Erin and Devin's home countless times; I have attended parties at their home; I have comforted him, Lance, and Alex following Erin's death, their beloved wife, mother, and sister-in-law. I have also worked closely with Devin in numerous charitable causes over the years.

Devin and Erin were extremely generous. They supported the Big Brother organization, college scholarships for needy high school graduates all over greater Los Angeles, homeless shelters, and food banks. Those are just the ones of which I have personal knowledge; no doubt, there were others. That was the kind of people they were. To my knowledge, none of these causes were done in secret. But one cause has always remained secret.

With Devin's death, I feel released from my promise to keep this aspect of his and Erin's generosity secret. He didn't ask that I carry this secret to my grave also. Thus, I think I can legitimately share what I'm going to say without violating my promise given so long ago. I do this also with Lance and Alex's permission.

In our church, we have a benevolence fund which Devin and Erin originally founded and funded. Our Fund assists not only our church members in crisis, but also assists many in need outside our church. Our assistance provides for many needs: unemployment assistance, paying bills, medical needs, et cetera. I and four Benevolence Fund board members distribute the funds by majority vote, but I can tell you our decisions have always been unanimous. In addition to creating it, Devin and Erin continued to be the major benefactors of our fund. I was until this moment the only person who knew about its origin and source of funding. Their contributions over the years created a successful avenue for assisting many in their time of need. Now everyone will know those primarily responsible for our fund.

Devin was a man who was living proof that from those who were given much, much was expected in return. What we do in our lives here on Earth is important. It is an outgrowth of our belief and faith in Jesus, and our effort to follow Him.

With every birth comes an appointment with death. Devin has met his appointment. No one escapes. It is in whom we believe and trust that determines our fate after death. Devin placed his belief and trust in Jesus and now receives his reward for a life of faith and service. He was the embodiment of "Love God" and "Love your neighbor as yourself."

Devin is not here today, only his body is. His soul has gone to be with Jesus. We are not here to shed tears, although we shed them. We are not here to mourn Devin's death, although we mourn. We are here to celebrate the race Devin has run, a race now won. Death was the end of his troubles, pain, sorrow, and fear.

I visited Devin a number of times before he died. He was responsive most of the time, and his humor was intact and engaged. I asked him how he was doing shortly after arriving on one of my last visits. His reply was, "Sam, you may have a better clue than I. I haven't read the Times today. If my name wasn't listed on the obituary pages, I'm doing well. If I am already listed there, I'm in bigger trouble than I think." I laughed but could only think Devin was not just being humorous; he didn't fear death, even though he didn't desire to leave those he loved. After his obituary page comment, he smiled and added, "Pastor, I think death may be nature's way of telling me to slow down." How like Devin to find humor in such moments. Many could not do that. At the conclusion of each visit with him, he asked me to pray with him, but he also asked me to pray over the coming months for Lance, Alexa, Christine, Mona and Ginny, his three business associates, Billy, Cliff, and Rick, their families, and all his friends and co-workers.

Devin was someone I respected, admired, and loved. I will miss him as will so many of you. Rest in peace, my friend, until we meet again.

Please join me now in prayer. Heavenly Father, as we leave this place bring comfort, as only you can, to all who are gathered here to celebrate the life of our departed loved one and friend. While Devin enjoys his new life in Heaven, we will miss him, but we know also that Heaven is promised to all who believe. In Jesus' name we pray.

As Pastor Sam resumed his seat, I rose, and walked to the lectern, more calmly and confidently than I'd thought possible. My prayers for strength had been answered. I looked out and smiled seeing so many of Mom and Dad's friends. I began:

My father was a good man but imperfect as are we all. His sister Alex and I lived with him all our lives so "this good and imperfect man" was very personal to us.

Many of you know that my parents were deeply religious. They maintained a faith in God and a belief in Christ from youth, even in the Hollywood environment where that was difficult, almost impossible sometimes. I'm forever thankful that my parents reared me in a religious home and provided for my religious foundation.

I'm one of the fortunate ones. I grew up in a home filled with love. There was never a moment when I didn't feel that love from Dad, and from Mom, but I also felt Mom and Dad's love for each other. That was good for me as a boy, but also a wonderful example for me as a young man.

In addition to religion, I was taught not only to be honest and to care, but also to give. I was taught that to those whom much is given, much is expected. I was taught to love and to forgive. And I was taught to dream. Dad and Mom had always held onto their dreams. I hold onto mine. There were no impossible dreams in our home.

You may wonder why I also speak of my mother on this occasion. That's because I couldn't say these words at my mom's service four years ago. I can say them now. I'll talk about both my parents. Dad would approve. I'm just a son who was blessed to have had them in his life. Dad and Mom are now in heaven. I say that with confidence.

My mother was a Christian. She was my first teacher, my nurse and caregiver, my listener, my advisor, and my friend. Mom loved and nurtured me, yet she also loved and nurtured others. She taught me how to love and about life, but she didn't teach me to cook.

Dad was fond of telling the story that after asking my grandparents for Mom's hand in marriage, my grandfather Brad had told him, "Devin, Alyssa and I have discussed the possibility of you and Erin marrying. While we have some reservations related to your career, we like you and the fact that you're a religious young fellow. We know you love Erin and she you. You have our permission; welcome to the family, Son. However, there's one word of caution, even if said in jest: Erin's a wonderful and beautiful young lady - I doubt you could have done better - but she's not the best cook and housekeeper you could have found. I hope you always have money to hire a cook and housekeeper."

Mom sometimes feigned anger about Dad telling that story, but Granddad Brad was right. My mom was a wonderful wife and mother, but she wasn't much of a cook. I'm grateful we had Mona in our house, and I know Dad was. Thank you, Mona, for coming along and keeping us from starving or living in a mess.

Those of you who knew my mother well know how much she detested dressing for and attending those required film premieres. On one such occasion she did something not generally known in the industry.

A few years ago, one of Dad's films was nominated for an Oscar. At the ceremony, a reporter asked Mom who had designed the dress she wore. Mom replied, "Oh, it's just a little Saint Pauli dress." The reporter said she'd never heard of Saint Pauli, to which Mom replied, "He's the top designer at Saint Paul's Thrift Shop. I just grabbed this thing off the rack, but I had it dry cleaned before tonight." Afterwards, Mom felt guilt about what she had said and sent a card apologizing for her tasteless and rude behavior.

How typical of my mother. She was a good and gracious lady, but she was more private than Dad. I still miss her.

While my mother was a private individual, my father was a public figure. Lots of information is known about him but not everything. An open book he was not. But I knew the private Devin MacArthur Bradshaw.

What can I say about my father? He was also a Christian, my teacher, my problem-solver, my listener, my advisor, and my friend. My dad's strong presence was always a comfort when I was sick, sad, or hurt. He could be difficult, though, when I did something wrong, so I avoided wrong as much as was humanly possible. But despite everything, said or unsaid, I always knew he loved me. How did I know? He told me, and he told me often, but I was certain by the way I was treated.

One of Dad's greatest attributes was that he was a hard worker. He did his job well, and thus, I learned to do the same.

Yes, Dad was a hard worker but something he said in one of his journals which I read a few days ago tells me just how important I was to him. I was about 6 on August 17, 1976, when he wrote:

I came home from the studio early yesterday afternoon. We had an early family meal because I had to return to the studio for an evening exterior shoot on the back lot. When I got ready to leave, I hugged and kissed Lance saying, "Daddy has to go back to work now. I love you."

Lance looked up at me sadly, and said, "Thanks for visiting us, Dad."

That was a blow. I couldn't stop the tears as I left the house to get into the car.

I knew at that moment I had to reduce my film work and spend more time with the family. After we wrap this film, I'm committed to doing that.

He fulfilled that commitment. Dad always attempted to place Mom before his career, a commitment he had made to my grandparents when he asked their permission to marry Mom. He made every effort to place both of us before his career, especially after what I had said to him. He did better than many husbands and fathers, I think. Mom and Dad had a good and solid marriage, an oddity in Hollywood.

I will think back on all the good talks we had, on all the advice, and on all the love. You may be gone physically, but your memory will remain with me forever.

Dad, even though you and Mom will never meet your future grandchildren, I pledge to you, I will rear them as I was reared.

And someday, I'm certain, we will all meet again. What a wonderful reunion we will have up there!

My final hours with Dad were spent holding his hand, talking to him, and praying. He was not communicative until the very end, but I talked to him anyway. At the end, he looked at me, recognized me, and said a few words meant only for me. Then, he smiled drawing his last breath. I knew he was meeting Mom and Jesus. Finally, he was in no pain and at peace; our long goodbye had ended. Somehow, that helped ease the pain of losing my dad, my friend.

I love you, Dad. I'll miss your kindness, your joy, and your advice to a son who always felt loved. Even though I'll miss you, I'll not say goodbye. I'll just say, "So long, Dad, until we meet again." And we will.

In closing, I will share one of Dad's favorite Bible passages, 1 Corinthians 13: If I speak in the tongues of men and of angels, but have not love, I am a noisy gong or a clanging cymbal. And if I have prophetic powers, and understand all mysteries and all knowledge, and if I have all faith, so as to remove mountains, but have not love, I am nothing. If I give away all I have, and if I deliver up my body to be burned, but have not love, I am nothing. Love is patient and kind; love does not envy or boast; it is not arrogant or rude. It does not insist on its own way; it is not irritable or resentful; it does not rejoice at wrongdoing, but rejoices with the truth. Love bears all things, believes all things, hopes all things, endures all things. Love never ends. As for prophecies, they will pass away; as for tongues, they will cease; as for knowledge, it will pass away. For we know in part and we prophesy in part, but when the perfect comes the partial will pass away. When I was a child I spoke like a child, I thought like a child, I reasoned like a child. When I became a man, I gave up childish ways. For now we see in a mirror dimly, but then face to face. Now I know in part; then I will know fully, even as I have been fully known. So now faith, hope, and love abide, these three; but the greatest of these is love.

I left the lectern, walked back toward my seat, but Aunt Alex had risen and met me near the casket. She embraced me, kissed me on the cheek, and whispered, "Lance, what you said about your parents was lovely." We resumed our seats as the choir began singing the piece of music also sung at the end of my mother's funeral, one often played and sung around our home piano, "The Impossible Dream." Granted, it was not a religious number, but one of our favorites.

The music and lyrics stirred and lifted my emotions, measure building upon measure, touching my soul from those first words until the last haunting line. I felt the piece a gift of God's love, just as is all music that touches the soul. Dad once told me, "The kind of music someone likes is a window into their soul." Hearing the music and lyrics transported my memories to Mom and Dad, playing and singing the piece around our piano, talking about our dreams, those met and those yet to fulfill. Those happy memories enabled me, at least in the moment, to forget sadness and focus on past happiness.

Following the service, we drove to the cemetery for the short graveside service. As soon as it concluded, Aunt Alex, Mona and her daughter Ginny, and I rose. We each placed a rose on Dad's casket. Mona and Ginny walked toward the waiting funeral home limo, while Alex and I stayed at the casket. Each of us, with a hand touching the casket, said a short prayer, then we kissed Dad's casket and walked toward the limo, our arms around each other. Neither of us shed any tears, both having shed too many in the previous days. Our tears were spent.

Cliff and Billy and their wives spoke brief words of condolence with us before we reached the limo. As we neared the car, Rick and his wife approached us.

Rick said, "Sue and I are so sorry for your loss. Your parents were indeed the individuals you said they were, Lance. We loved them. Devin was my lifelong friend. We'll all miss him."

"Thanks, Rick, for everything. I'll call if I have any additional questions. And thanks for bringing out to the house the things Dad left for me." We shook hands, and Rick and Sue turned and walked toward their car.

As I turned to move on to the limo, I heard a slightly-accented voice from behind me say, "Mr. Bradshaw, could I have a brief moment?"

I turned. Before me stood an elegant older woman entirely dressed in a black, tailored suit, large-brimmed hat, veil, stockings, and heels. She had that sophisticated, European look. I walked toward the soothing, compelling voice.

While I couldn't place the accent, she appeared to be someone interesting. I said, "Yes, could I help you?"

"I'm sorry to intrude at a time like this, but it is important. You do not know me, but we have a connection through your father."

"What sort of connection?"

"My name is Valentina DeLuca Taylor."

"I know the name."

"How is that possible?"

"You're Anna's mother and Christine's grandmother. You're mentioned in Dad's journals and in a letter to Dad from the detective agency."

"A detective agency?"

"Yes, Dad's been searching for Anna and Christine for decades. He always wanted to see his daughter again. I was asked to find her."

"We didn't know."

"Are Anna and Christine here with you?"

"No unfortunately, they are not. They are in London, but they know I'm attending your father's funeral service today. I am in Los Angeles for a meeting about my granddaughter's future and read your father's obituary in the <u>Times</u>. I stayed on for his service and to possibly meet you."

"Will you put me in contact with Christine?"

"I think I can make that happen," she said smiling. "I'm staying at the Beverly Hills Hotel on Sunset. Could we meet in the next few days?"

"I could meet you there in the morning."

"About 9:30 or so would be perfect. We will have breakfast together. Just inquire at the desk, and they will direct you to my bungalow. I'll notify the desk you will be asking for me. Thank you."

She turned and walked across the lawn. I'd read she'd been a famous model in her younger days. That was evident by her graceful movement. Watching as she entered a limo parked not far away, I momentarily felt a wave of excitement, anticipation regarding tomorrow. This woman was the key I needed to reach Christine. My adoption and Dad were momentarily forgotten.

Chapter Fifteen

Devin's Journal, Wednesday, June 3, 1964

The past seems to arise from the ashes at the most inopportune time. My situation now. I've heard from Anna after all these years.

Sunday, May 24, 1964

Dear Devin,

Yes, I found your address. Rather, a friend did.

I'm so happy for your success in films. I've read your movie is wonderful. I can't wait to see it. You'll never know how happy I'll be to watch you on that screen and read about your future successes. Not much manages to get into print about you though, but I know you are a private kind of guy. No doubt, you're guarding your privacy as always. I did see a picture of you with your wife recently at some movie opening. She's a lovely and lucky woman. You must love her very much to have made that commitment. My best wishes.

About six years ago, I told you I'd contact you eventually. I'm keeping that promise now. You noted, no doubt, no return address on the envelope. Once again I'm asking that you make no effort to contact me for safety reasons. You respected my wish years ago, so I expect you will respect it this time also.

The "wonderful gift" you left me is now five years old, a daughter I named Christine. She's a lovely girl who looks somewhat like a female version of you, with curly blonde hair and brown eyes, and is rather tall for her age. I love her deeply. She's the part of you I got to keep. I thank you for that. She's my life now. We have a good life, but not the one I'd have hoped.

I have no idea whether you ever suspected that I left the university because I was pregnant. I know you had lots of guilt about our night together, but please have no regret about our daughter. You can be proud of her. Knowing your religious views, I am confident that once you meet her, you will know she's a blessing. As you said to me once, "God works all things for good." She is the good, believe me! My father would be extremely unhappy if he knew about this contact and what I am proposing. Just accept things as they must be. Please. I beg you.

I'll have Christine at the top of the Empire State Building Saturday, June 13. Please be there to get her. And feel free to bring your wife. I'd like to meet her. Christine will be able to spend about eight hours on Saturday and again on Sunday with you and your wife. That's all I can safely permit. Christine loves Central Park so take her there. She loves ice cream. And she loves movies and Broadway shows. Enjoy your time with her. In many ways, she's a chip off the "old block."

Christine's been told her father is a very busy man, and that he has a wife named Erin. Please just tell her you're "Daddy." I've told her you will be coming to visit her, and she's very excited about that. Please don't disappoint her; she'd be hurt.

You may wonder why I selected the observation deck at the top of the Empire State Building. If you've ever seen the Deborah Kerr, Cary Grant movie, <u>An Affair to Remember</u>, I'm sure you'll understand why I selected that as the meeting place.

Again, Christine and I will be there at 10 a.m. on Saturday, June 13 and again on Sunday, June 14. We'll wait for thirty minutes.

My best,
Anna

Erin and I spent much of the evening discussing Anna's letter. We agree we must meet Christine. Tomorrow, I'll book our flight to New York and the hotel reservation. While I have mixed feelings about this, I must meet my daughter.

I find it rather interesting that Anna has never contacted me regarding support. I'd have accepted my responsibility gladly. I can only assume there's good reason I was never asked.

Erin's Diary, Monday, June 15, 1964

The weekend in New York with Christine was difficult for Dev, for both of us really. Christine is a lovely little girl. One look at her, and it's clear she's Dev's child. I enjoyed our time with her. Being a part of a man I love, I have to love her, but she's so easy to love. She makes me feel warm. Just to have a child of my own, our own! A child would make our life perfect.

I feel so sorry for Dev. The weekend was an emotional one. After Anna took Christine following our hours together, all Dev could do was cry in my arms. He has much love to give. His sadness is twofold. On the one hand, he knows Christine needs a father's love; on the other, Dev needs Christine's love. For having never seen him before, she seemed comfortable with him after a few hours. I wonder what Anna has told her all these years when the questions came. Surely there were questions. Maybe we'll never know. Christine's too young for that discussion. I know Dev longs for more visits with Christine.

Anna's story is a mystery to us.

Devin's Journal, Tuesday, June 16, 1964

We flew into New York/JFK on the 12th and took a limo to the Plaza Hotel where I'd booked us. We wanted to be close to Central Park.

At 10 a.m. on Saturday the 13th Erin and I walked out on the observation deck. As we walked around to our right Erin poked me and pointed. Just ahead of us was Anna speaking to a little girl and pointing to some distance place. She must have sensed our presence because Anna turned, smiled, took the child by the hand, and walked the short distance between us saying, "You're on time."

"Of course we are. We wouldn't be late."

Anna extended her hand to Erin saying, "I'm Anna, and you're Erin. I've seen your picture. I'm glad to meet you."

"And I'm glad to meet you," Erin responded.

Anna looked down to the child and said, "Christine, this is your father and his wife, Erin."

"Hello," the child said, "I'm glad to meet you." She extended her hand to me and then to Erin. I assumed she had been primed but wasn't certain. She turned back to her mother, "What do I call him, Mommy?"

"Christine," I said, "just call me Daddy and my wife, Erin. Is that okay?"

"Yes. I like that."

"Where are you staying?" Anna asked.

"We're at The Plaza to be close to Central Park."

"Then I'll leave Christine with you and pick her up before 6 p.m. in the hotel lobby. Okay?"

"That's fine."

"Christine, I'm going now. Your Daddy and Erin will take you to Central Park. I'll see you at six. Is that okay?"

"Mommy, do I have to go with them without you?"

Noting Christine's reluctance to go with strangers, Erin said, "Anna, please spend the rest of the day with us. Christine needs to get to know her father and me. I'm sure she'd like you to come with us."

"Please, Mommy?" Christine begged.

"Erin, are you sure you and Devin are comfortable with my doing that?"

"Anna," I said, "we're fine with your spending the day with us. Christine needs to get to know us. Perhaps tomorrow, she'll be more comfortable. Would you like for your mommy to stay, Christine?"

"Yes. Please, Mommy."

"Then if no one minds, it's a plan," Anna said a bit less convincingly. Anna probably sounded more convincing to Christine than to Erin and me.

"Now the four of us are off for the day." I knelt down and said to Christine, "Would you like to spend the day in Central Park or go to a play? Daddy can get tickets to <u>Hello Dolly</u>.

"Mommy's talked about that play. Central Park tomorrow?"

"Yes, Christine. Let's get something to eat before the play."

We took a taxi to the Plaza. I stopped at the concierges desk and requested four tickets to <u>Hello Dolly</u>; then we went on to The Palm Court for lunch.

After lunch we taxied to the St. James Theatre on 44th for the matinee.

As we entered the taxi following the play, Christine said, "Daddy, the play was good. I liked that Dolly lady."

"Yes, she was good, Christine," Erin said.

"Where do you live, Daddy?"

"We live in California. That's a long way from here."

"Will I see you again?"

What could I say? "I'll see you tomorrow and will come see you whenever I can. I'm very busy and live a long way from here."

"Mommy says that. Don't you, Mommy?"

"Yes, honey. Your daddy is a very busy man and lives a long way from New York."

"Christine, do you still want to go to Central Park tomorrow?" Erin asked her.

"Walk in the park and see the zoo."

"Okay, that's what we'll do."

We left the taxi and entered the hotel lobby. I noticed Anna looking at her watch. She turned to us and said, "I'm sorry, but we need to be on our way now. I'll have her at the same place in the morning at ten."

We tried to hide our disappointment, but I said, "Erin and I will see you in the morning, Christine. We had lots of fun. Could I have a hug now?"

"Yes, Daddy." She moved toward me, and I knelt, picked her up, and hugged her tightly.

"Thanks for a wonderful day, Christine. And thank you, Anna. We'll see you in the morning."

I put her down, and she turned to Erin and said, "I'll hug you too. Okay?"

"Yes, honey, it is." Erin hugged her, but I noticed tears welling in Erin's eyes as Christine moved to Anna.

"I'm sorry we have to rush off so quickly, but we'll see you in the morning," Anna said.

As they moved across the lobby to the front doors, I pulled Erin close as we watched them pass through the doors and onto the sidewalk.

"She's lovely, Dev. Today went well, even with Anna along. I can't help wishing Christine were ours."

"I know. She's mine, but she's not mine. I want her with us. Why are things like this?" Neither of us had an answer.

On Sunday morning we picked up Christine as planned. She was eager to go without Anna. We taxied to Central Park. The day was bittersweet for me, probably also for Erin. I knew that late in the afternoon Christine would be gone again without my knowing when I'd see her again.

It was such a joy to see her happiness at the zoo. She'd probably seen all the animals before, but she still loved visiting again. We ate hot dogs for lunch, followed by chocolate ice cream cones. Then it was back to more of the zoo.

We returned to the hotel lobby with a few minutes to spare and found Anna waiting.

Erin hugged Christine goodbye while I thanked Anna and asked, "When can I spend more time with Christine?"

"When I can arrange it, Devin! Please don't ask for information I can't give you now."

"Anna, why does it have to be like this?"

"Devin, please don't ask."

I recognized the finality in her voice and replied, "Okay. Whatever." This situation was exasperating.

I hugged Christine and said, "I love you."

"Daddy, I love you too. Thanks for all the fun. Bye."

We overheard Christine ask Anna as they were heading away, "When can I see Daddy and Erin again?" We could see Anna reply, but they were beyond our hearing range.

All I could do when Erin and I reached our room was cry as Erin held me. She cried too, but perhaps more out of sympathy for me.

"This situation needs to be different!"

"I know, Dev."

Since we've returned to Malibu, each time I think of Christine, tears well in my eyes. How long will this go on?

I know one thing. I'm hiring a private detective to search for them. Erin has encouraged me to do that.

Devin's Journal, Monday, October 3, 1966

At Erin's insistence, I'd hired a private investigating firm in June 1964. Their assignment was to locate Anna and Christine. Yesterday, after a wait of two years, the investigator called to say his report was being sent over by private courier. It was in my hands in about two hours or so.

Gerald A. Hanford, Private Investigations

Investigation and Detective Service Company

1001 Business Plaza on Wilshire Boulevard, Suite 705

Los Angeles, California 90017

September 30, 1966

Mr. and Mrs. Bradshaw:

My investigation as of this date into the whereabouts of one Anna Christine Taylor and her daughter Christine has resulted in the following initial findings:

1. New York birth records were located for both Miss Taylor and daughter Christine Ann.

2. Christine Ann's last name is listed as Taylor on her birth certificate.

3. Miss Taylor's father Robert is the lead attorney with Taylor and Taylor law firm, a successful Manhattan firm, by the way, founded by his father years ago.

4. Mr. Taylor's father practiced in the firm with his son until he and his wife were mysteriously gunned down in their Long Island home last year. Crime unsolved.

5. As you may or may not deduce from #4, Taylor and Taylor represents some clients thought involved in organized crime. My professional opinion after interviewing my contacts within the law enforcement community is that many of the firm's clients are such types.

6. Miss Taylor's maternal grandparents' last known address was in Milan, Italy. They no longer reside at that address.

7. Miss Taylor's mother, Valentina DeLuca Taylor, divorced her father this year in Las Vegas citing infidelity, mental and physical abuse, emotional distress, and irreconcilable differences. A few days after the divorce decree was granted, the mother fled the country.

8. Mrs. Valentina Taylor had been a well-known fashion model in Milan prior to coming to NYC to work. There she met and married Mr. Robert Taylor.

9. I suspect she is now in a remote section of Italy, perhaps with her parents, the DeLuca's. We could not trace her or them beyond a location in Rome about six months ago. I am confident her family has sufficient means and connections, not only to hide her, but also to see that she and the family are well protected.

10. With the ex-husband's possible criminal connections, she may well have reason to fear for her safety.

11. The last known address for Miss Taylor and daughter Christine was an apartment on Park Avenue. We cannot find a trace since they vacated that apartment three months ago.

12. We may be dealing with a potentially dangerous father considering his possible criminal connections and the divorce records.

13. I suggest we tread lightly in the future so as to assure we leave no footprints. We must consider you and your own family's safety.

Mr. and Mrs. Bradshaw, I'm sorry to report that we seem to have reached a dead-end at this point. I will continue to pursue tracking them and will inform you immediately if and when I have new developments.

As per your original instructions, I will continue to send any additional invoices for our services to your accountant, Mr. Clifton Dunne.

If at any point you desire we cease tracking the aforementioned individuals, or if you have questions, please contact me.

Sincerely,
Gerry

Erin and I both think the report a bit ominous, both for Anna and Christine, and perhaps for us. Could we be in some danger?

Devin's Journal, Friday, June 13, 1969

Finally, another letter from Anna has arrived, welcomed, yet unwelcome. I long to see Christine again, but I know it's to be immense happiness followed by pain. I have to play this "game," otherwise, I don't see Christine. She needs a father in her life. No further word from the private detective agency though.

June 9, 1969
Devin and Erin,

Five more years have passed since I last wrote you. It's been a difficult five years for us, but we are both well thanks to my mother and close friends. We manage to see my Italian grandparents on the sly, a miracle in our lives.

Christine's now ten, and she's still a lovely girl. I'm sure she'll always be.

She's looking forward to seeing you both. You and Erin will have two days again with her if all goes as planned. No, don't ask why. Just accept what has to be without questions. Please. I assure you it's best for all of us.

We'll be in the same place as five years ago at 10 a.m. on Saturday, July 5, 1969. As before, we'll wait thirty minutes.

See you,
Anna

P.S. If for some reason we are not there just know it isn't because we didn't want to be; it's a safety issue.

Neither Erin nor I know exactly what all this meant, but we have to assume it has something to do with Anna's father. I fear for Anna and Christine. Erin and I will probably be fine with the security we have.

Devin's Journal, July 8, 1969

We're both sad. The tears I've shed in the last few days have not really made me feel better, but I shed them anyway. There's no assurance of future visits with Christine. The two days we spent with her were wonderful, but they ended. Why? It's bizarre, in addition to being unfair.

Christine is a sweet and loving child. I have to credit Anna for that. Our visit was over too soon though.

Malibu seems a sadder place for me now. Will this ever end? I want to see her again.

Devin's Journal, Tuesday, May 19, 1992

Gerry called yesterday morning saying he was sending his latest search findings over by courier. I got them late yesterday afternoon. Alex signed for the letter and brought it to me. I read and placed it in my center desk drawer where Lance would find it. Gerry thinks he has a good lead on the whereabouts of Valentina DeLuca Taylor. He is convinced Anna's father had some involvement in Erin's accident based on information two Los Angeles detectives provided him. Why didn't the detectives inform me?

Lance will have to take it from here.

I know my end is near; I'm just too tired and sick to deal with this development. My winter is approaching. I'm much like flowers or leaves on a tree. The flowers bloom in spring, but slowly dry. Leaves begin to fall as winter approaches. My flowers have dried; my leaves are falling.

Chapter Sixteen

June 21, 1992

Sleep didn't come easily last evening. I was awake off and on during the night. Anticipation about my meeting this morning with Anna's mother kept invading my thoughts; yet I'd taken the first step in fulfilling Dad's last request.

I rose early, grabbed my bath robe, and went down to the kitchen. Mona usually didn't arrive at the house until about seven-thirty or so. Aunt Alex was obviously still sleeping since I hadn't heard her. The house remained quiet as I made coffee and went into the study. The strong coffee had a welcome taste and helped me recover from an evening of tossing.

I had already read Dad's journals and Mom's diaries, but read more carefully those parts related to Anna and Christine, as well as the two letters from Gerry Hanford, the private investigator Dad had hired decades ago.

I was immediately struck by Mr. Hanford's comments in his first letter about Robert Taylor's connections, his parents having been gunned down in their home, and Mr. Hanford's warning about our family's safety. Those statements hadn't impacted me as much during my first reading.

Mom's accident had never been fully explained. The police investigation seemed to end in a roadblock. Could her accident have been arranged as a warning to Dad? Mr. Hanford seems to think Anna's father is responsible according to the information he has received from his LAPD contacts. Would an arranged hit have come almost twenty years after Dad and Mom had last visited with Christine? Why not earlier? Could it have been pay-

back for Dad's last meeting with Christine and Anna? Did something occur four or five years ago? The thoughts were disturbing.

Before seven, I went upstairs, shaved, showered, and dressed.
Well before nine, I was on the highway headed for The Beverly
Hills Hotel. Once at the hotel, I inquired at the desk for Ms.
Taylor's bungalow.

I arrived at her door just as breakfast was being delivered. As
she answered the door, she saw me approaching and waved.

She was more informally dressed than I'd expected. Her hair
had been pulled back into a pony-tail. Her pony-tail and floral
print, silk blouse, white slacks, and high heels contributed to
her youthful look. She seemed much younger than I'd expected.
Yesterday the veil had partially hidden her facial features. I had
calculated her age as in her early seventies, but obviously she
was well-preserved. She either had great genes or had been the
recipient of a skilled plastic surgeon's services.

"Mr. Bradshaw," she began, "take a seat at the table; we will
enjoy our breakfast, make small talk as you Americans are so
fond of saying, and then get into some substance. I hope bacon,
eggs, and English muffins are satisfactory?"

"That would be great, but please call me, Lance."

"Wonderful, young man. Lance, please call me, Val. First
names make me feel younger anyway."

Small talk it was over breakfast, nothing much except the
weather in California, Italy, and other European spots, plus visits
to Paris and Rome we'd each made in the past. I was grateful to
have vacationed with Mom and Dad in Europe a few times, so I
wasn't a completely uninformed, ugly American.

After breakfast, Val said, "Lance, let us take our coffee to the
sofa and armed chair. Both are more comfortable. She stretched
on the sofa and indicated I should take the chair.

"Lance, my granddaughter waited a long time to meet her father again."

"Val, it's been over two decades. Christine was ten years old the last time Dad saw her. Now she'll never see him again. I'm sad for both of them."

"We are all too aware of that. However, it could not be avoided. Anna felt it necessary for everyone's safety."

"Why is that?"

"There were dangers to everyone. We might have all been hurt or worse."

"Are you aware that my mother was killed in an unsolved auto accident four years ago? Dad's private detective thinks he has evidence your ex-husband is responsible."

"Her death made the news, even in Europe. My friend here in Los Angeles, also shared what information was available to him, mostly what was available in the media or items he picked up from his Hollywood connections. We were sorry to hear about your mother. I would not be shocked if my ex were involved. What your detective's sources tell him may well be true. I have no proof it is, but I suspect it might be. Permit me to tell you a little about my family."

"Please do. Dad didn't have a lot of information."

"I am the daughter of Francine and Roberto DeLuca of Milan. You know of our family?"

"I'm sorry to say, I don't."

"My parents founded the DeLuca Fashion House of Milan many decades ago. As a teenager I began modeling their designs. In my early twenties, I also modeled in Paris, Rome, London, Sydney, Hollywood, and New York. In addition to fashion modeling, I had a varied career in print and television ads for a variety of beauty products. While working in New York, I met Robert

Taylor, a flashy, rather charismatic, successful lawyer who was a partner in his father's legal firm. I married him after a whirlwind romance as you Americans might call it. He was handsome, charming, and attentive, but I later discovered beautifully wrapped packages sometimes contain an abhorrent gift. Anna was born two years later. He was a good husband and father for many years, but long before Anna went off to the University of Arizona we lived with an abusive man."

"I recall Dad's journal mentioned Anna's grandparents having a condo in Tucson."

"Robert's parents did, not mine. They called themselves New York snowbirds. I thought that a humorously-bizarre expression. Anna wanted out of the house; I wanted her away at college. While reluctant, Robert finally permitted her to enroll at Arizona."

"Why Arizona?"

"It was as far away from Robert as I could get her, and his parents wintered there. Well before Anna went off to the university my husband was flaunting serial affairs with almost anything wearing a skirt. He was also drinking heavily, was possibly using drugs, had a violent and dangerous temper, and was threatening both me and Anna. Needless to say, our marriage was in trouble, and Anna and I faced danger. Are you aware of Robert's unfortunate connections?"

"I read something sent to Dad years ago from the detective agency about possible criminal connections."

"Let's just call them bad men, all sorts of them. Many were extremely dangerous. Representing them made Robert and his father wealthy. That wealth came at a steep price as so often happens with what some might say were ill-gotten gains. Robert's parents were killed in their Long Island home, probably as a warning to Robert. In the mid-1960s, I divorced Robert and fled to Italy. Robert was not a happy man. Thankfully, my parents were able to provide protection and keep me hidden. We also have a few unsavory types in Italy who can be bought for a price. We were well protected."

"And Anna and Christine stayed in New York?"

"They did against my advice. Robert hid them somewhere in upstate New York or Canada, but they called me often, always being cautious. Also, I periodically saw them surreptitiously."

"Why did Dad never see Christine after she was ten?"

"Robert somehow found out about their last meeting. He was supposed to be in Europe. Anna thought she was always careful. It was then that Robert discovered the name of Christine's father. Anna had always refused to tell him your father's name. How he found out then, we don't know."

"Why had she never told her father?"

"She knew he had a violent temper. He had made threats against Christine's father without even knowing his name. Once Robert found out Christine's father's name, he made even more serious threats. Anna agreed Christine would never see her father again, and in exchange Robert promised never to harm your parents."

"Why did she trust him?"

"Anna had no choice but to trust at that point. Regarding your mother's accident, all we have are suspicions, but your detective probably has evidence."

"Did something change in 1988 when my mother died?"

"We don't know. Robert got remarried after our divorce to some crime boss's daughter. She was shot on a Manhattan street in 1988. Perhaps that caused him to act."

"And has something changed now? Why are you in America?"

"Yes, something has changed. My ex-husband was killed six months ago. Shot by a client. It seems Robert was having an affair with the client's wife?"

"Was the client involved in criminal activity?"

"I have no proof of that, just a suspicion. Many of his clients were though. The police may have proof."

"So, Anna is now free?"

"Yes, free in one sense, but never free from the years of fear."

"And also Christine?"

"Yes."

"What's Christine done all these years?"

"She has been modeling and acting, of course, all under the name of Francine Rossi. My granddaughter is a beautiful and talented young woman. She has good genes from both parents it seems."

"And you're in Hollywood to help Christine's career?"

"Yes, but my friend hasn't been of much help to date."

"What does Christine want? A movie career?"

"Yes."

"Would you be interested in a meeting with Dad's agent, Billy Feldmann?"

"You could arrange that?"

"I'm certain I could. Dad would want me to do that for her."

"Oh, young man, how can I ever thank you?"

"By bringing Christine here or telling me where I can find her."

"Are you free in a week?"

"I can arrange that."

"Then you fly to New York with me in a few days. Anna and Christine will meet us there."

"That's great. Now, would you permit me to use the phone?"

"Definitely."

I rose, picked up the phone on a nearby table, and dialed Billy at home. Two rings later, I heard Billy's familiar answer, "Feldmann residence."

"Billy, this is Lance."

"How are you, son?"

"I'm doing better, especially now. I need a huge favor."

"How can I help you? Are you finally interested in film acting?"

"No, but I know someone who is. That's why I called. Are you available to meet me in an hour or so?"

"I can do that. At your house?"

"No, at the Beverly Hills Hotel on Sunset."

"Why there?"

"You'll see, Billy. When you get to the desk just ask for Valentina DeLuca Taylor's bungalow."

"Who's she? A girlfriend?"

"No, she isn't. You'll find out when you get here."

Since Billy lived off Coldwater Canyon Drive in Beverly Hills, he was in the bungalow in less than an hour. After introductions, Val ordered more coffee, and we sat.

Billy looked at me and said, "Okay, Lance what's this all about?"

"Dad's daughter, Christine, is a model and actress. Val is her grandmother."

"You're joking?"

"No, I'm not."

"Wait a minute. Your dad asked Rick to add a Christine to his will at the last meeting all of us had with him, and a daughter was mentioned in Devin's obituary. I chose not to inquire at that time. I didn't want to pry, but probably would have done so later."

"That's the Christine. Would you be interested in possibly representing Christine?"

"That depends. Does she have any talent?"

"Mr. Feldmann, I can assure you my granddaughter has talent and is beautiful. Would you care to look at her resume, portfolio, and a video?"

"I would."

Val brought out the resume and portfolio and handed them to Billy. She had inserted the video while Billy had driven over.

As Billy went through them, we could hear him mutter, "Wow! She's stunning!" He looked up and said to Val, "I think I've seen her in some perfume ads."

"You probably have, Mr. Feldmann. She does photo advertisements in addition to acting."

"She resembles Devin."

I'd had the same thought as I'd looked over Billy's shoulder at a few of the shots. Christine was indeed stunning.

"Ms. Taylor, do you have a video with you of Christine's work?"

"I do, and I have it ready to play. What I'll show you are some scenes from a recent movie Christine made in Australia." She stood back as the images began to roll on the screen.

I found watching the scenes intriguing. Billy's reaction was much more guarded. As the video ended, Billy said, "Ms. Taylor, would you lend me the video, portfolio, and resume for a few days. I'd like to show these to a few people out at Crossroads."

"That's her father's studio isn't it, Mr. Feldmann?"

"Yes, it was Devin's studio. I think they'd have an interest in Devin's daughter."

"Mr. Feldmann, I'll be here a few more days on other business. Then, Lance and I are flying to New York to meet Christine and my daughter."

"I'll have these back to you in a few days. Thanks for calling me, Lance. This will be interesting. Devin's daughter's an actress. Wow!"

After Billy left, Val and I made our New York flight reservations, and I made my departure. This would be of interest to Aunt Alex, I knew.

After I'd told Alex about my meeting with Val, she said, "Lance, you're finding locating Christine easier than you thought possible a few days ago. Finding your biological family may prove more difficult."

"I know, and that bugs me. I feel drawn to locating my birth mother. Why I'm not sure, but I need a plan. Perhaps we need to go to the library and do some research."

"I'm up to that task, Lance."

The next day I walked along the beach, thinking. I felt almost as though my entire being was now defined by the loss of my father and the fact that I was adopted. Maybe that feeling would pass with time.

That afternoon as I sat on the sand watching the waves roll in, I became mesmerized by the sea gulls. They circled overhead and periodically came in for a landing on the wet sand, an unending cycle, a pattern that continued regardless of what happened along the beach. The world in which I now lived had turned upside down, while the sea gulls' world always seemed to stay in balance. Instantly, Aunt Alex's comment struck me. "This is a bump in the road. Life continues." I had another family, a family I needed to locate, if only to help me fully understand who I am. I'd soon meet Christine, so that hurdle was almost complete.

All my life I thought I was home. I thought I knew who I was. Maybe I was never really home. Maybe I didn't know who I was, only thought I did. My parents loved me, and I loved them, but perhaps I was never home. Now that Dad and Mom are gone I feel as a bird must, soaring above, looking for its nest, its home, but it's not to be found, as if it'd been destroyed for some reason. Where is my home, especially now that I know I am adopted?

I grew up thinking I was normal. I now know I'm different. I'll always be adopted. It'll never be behind me.

Had I known all along I was adopted, would I have felt differently about Mom and Dad? Most babies grow in a mother's womb; instead, I grew in my mother's heart, and in Dad's also. I felt grateful realizing the love I'd always had was more than many kids ever have.

I know adoption is about love. I had felt it. However, I now also know adoption is about pain. I feel that pain. I'm different. I know my other family is out there. Somewhere. Was that what I'd always felt was missing? Christine was family also, but that situation was different.

The questions about my other family swirl in my mind. They haunt me. Who are these people? What do they look like? Am I like them? Why did they "give me away"? Having answers would be better than these questions.

I got out of bed the next day, a few days before leaving for New York, knowing this was the day I would begin my search. When I came down for breakfast, I told Alex that I was ready to begin.

She suggested once we reached the library we not only look for books on adoption, but especially for those about how to do a search. Of course, I could hire a detective, but knew I needed this search diversion after Dad's death. This, I wanted to do personally.

Alex and I checked out a number of library books which appeared promising. After a day of research and making notes, we had many search suggestions. Some we discarded for the time being, but we settled on one that might prove promising, contacting the Seattle agency through which I was adopted and asking them to serve as an intermediary to my birth parents. Thus, I drafted and mailed a letter.

To Whom It May Concern:

On September 5, 1970, I was adopted as a newborn and my placement was through your agency. I am now of legal age and find there is a need for more information regarding my background and heritage than my parents were provided at the time of my adoption.

I am aware of the policy and practice in adoption to protect privacy by keeping identities secret, but I feel that it is in my interest and welfare to make contact.

An adoptee's interest should be paramount in all adoption cases.

I hereby formally request that your office serve as an intermediary between me and my birth parents. I am aware that other agencies are now doing this for adoptees of legal age, and it is permitted by law. Should there be a fee for this service, please notify me, and I will promptly forward payment.

I waive confidentiality and grant permission to the agency to share my name and address with my birth parents, but request that you notify me when contact is made and my personal information is shared. I also ask that you request my birth parents contact me at their convenience.

My sincere appreciation for your efforts.

Sincerely,
Lance Evan Bradshaw

P.S. I am enclosing under separate cover a letter and some pictures to my birth mother assuming she is the birth parent more likely to respond favorably to my request herein. Please forward my letter to her.

The letter I enclosed to my birth mother read:

Dear _____,

I am sorry to begin in that manner, but I do not know how to address you. "Birth mother" seems strange. Forgive me, but I cannot say, "Mom" or "Mother." I had a mom and mother. She loved me, reared me, and I loved her. I mean no disrespect; it's just that I feel the need for another term or a name, but I have none at present. I'm sorry about that.

I want you to know I am thankful to have been given life. I have no anger about being placed for adoption. My adopted family loved me deeply. I understand fully there are many times in life when we have little control over what we must do. Sometimes we have to make difficult decisions. We do the best we can under the circumstances.

I had terrific parents who reared me properly, and provided me with a wonderful life. My mother never worked after I came into my parents' lives. Unfortunately, my mother died in an auto accident a number of years ago, while my father just recently died of cancer. I miss them. My father was an actor in Hollywood. You would know him by his professional name, Devin MacArthur. Both were wonderful individuals and terrific parents. I loved them deeply.

You might have an interest in seeing some photos. I have included many covering various stages in my life, some alone, and others with one or both of my parents.

I would enjoy hearing from you when, and if, you are ready to take that step.

Sincerely,
Lance Evan Bradshaw

Enclosures: Photos

Chapter Seventeen

June 29, 1992

Once I'd mailed the letters to the adoption agency, I kept thinking this would prove futile, or worse, traumatic. Maybe neither of my birth parents would want contact. Aunt Alex and I had read about adoptees searching, only to have disappointing results: that one or both the birth parents were deceased, that the birth parents wanted no contact, that an adoptee had been removed from an abusive home. On and on the list of possible negative results went. So I'd gone into this search with my eyes open. At least, I thought they were open. I continued to believe that knowing was better than not knowing, but would I think that if I received negative responses? I wasn't certain. My parents had taught me nothing comes our way without us having the strength to deal with it. I just hoped I had that strength.

When Billy had returned Christine's video and portfolio to Val, he said there was interest in Christine at the studio, but he would contact her directly.

As planned, Val and I flew into JFK early on June 29 and took a limo into Manhattan. She dropped me off at The Plaza where we'd always stayed on family trips to the city and went on to the Waldorf where she said she'd always stayed.

Anna and Christine were due to arrive from London early the next afternoon. My evening was free as Val was meeting modeling friends. As the show was about a month from the end of its run, I got tickets to see the revival of <u>Man of La Mancha</u>. I'd never seen the show performed before and couldn't spend an evening alone in my hotel room when I had a chance to see the musical which had made "The Impossible Dream" popular.

The show was a treat for me. Memories around our family piano singing "The Impossible Dream" and many other songs flooded me. Happy memories they were.

Val had told me that Anna and Christine's flight tomorrow from London was due in shortly after lunch. To give them time to get settled, she'd invited me to come to her room about five for dinner.

I spent part of the next morning walking in Central Park, but the images of Mom and Dad's pictures with Christine in the park kept intruding. I thought it so sad Dad hadn't seen his daughter after age ten, about twenty-three years ago. How sad for both of them.

Leaving Central Park, I walked down Broadway recalling the last time, about six years before, Mom, Dad, and I had spent a few days in the city seeing shows. At 44th I walked over to 5th Avenue. While I purchased little, I did enjoy looking in a few stores as I wound my way back to The Plaza to dress for dinner.

A few minutes after five, I was admitted to Val's room carrying Dad's journals in a bag. Following introductions, we had dinner in the room. As in Los Angeles, there was little conversation of substance.

Anna, like her mother, was a beautiful woman. I partially understood Dad being interested in her; she was blonde, like Mom, and must have been stunning as a young college student.

Christine seemed an interesting person, plus she was a beautiful gal, a bit shy, but she physically was a captivating combination of her mother, grandmother, and Dad. She appeared to be a rather delicate female, lean and small boned. In many ways she was a blonde female version of Dad, except for her brown eyes and standing only about 5'10" tall. Her slender figure made her perfect for modeling, but it was her alluring face which made her perfect for perfume and cologne ads. A camera would love that face. Both males and females would be drawn to her face as they turned magazine pages.

As we concluded our meal, Val rose and said, "I regret leaving you now, but I must dress to go out.

After we heard the bedroom door close, Anna looked at me and said, "Lance, you will be able to talk with Christine after my mother and I leave for the evening. We're meeting old friends. I want to share some things about your father and me first. Okay?"

"Dad mentions you in his journals, but I certainly want to hear the story from you."

"My life brings back emotions I prefer to leave behind, but I must share them with you."

"I have all evening, Anna. Rest assured, I understand leaving emotions behind. I have memories which haunt me."

"Devin taught me many things. I wasn't religious when we met over thirty years ago, but I now attend church regularly because of the influence he had on me, plus influence from my husband. Even though Devin and I had a short romance, I loved him. He was easy to love and so unlike my father. My father was an angry, controlling, and abusive man especially by the time I left home for Tucson and the university; he was difficult to love. Devin wasn't. He was kind. He liked to maintain personal control but was never controlling. I knew he didn't love me but did enjoy my company. I also knew we had no future together. I longed for one with him. I was young, immature, and I wanted to hang onto him, but Devin was intent on having a future in acting, not a marriage. I have no doubt that had I stayed and told him I was pregnant, he would have married me, but I couldn't bring myself to do that to him. Thankfully, I was not that selfish, even though it was a disservice to both him and Christine. I'm the guilty one. Yes, I enticed him, but I had no regrets at the time. While I later had regrets, Christine is the part of Devin I got to keep. I don't regret her; she was my life until I married. Without her I couldn't have survived my father. She was a blessing and the good I think God creates from something He wouldn't support or approve. That 'good from bad' was your dad's philosophy."

"Yes, Dad always believed God could and did use something bad to create good."

"I always wanted Christine to grow up knowing her father and having a relationship with him. Instead, my father prevented that. My mother endured a lot of pain as long as she stayed with him. When she left, I should have taken Christine and gone also. I was afraid for your family and my own, and probably rightfully so. Staying was stupid of me in some ways, but I don't regret trying to protect our families, even if Christine was denied her father."

"I understand, Anna."

"On those two occasions when Christine was five and ten with my father supposedly out of the country, I contacted Devin and your mother to visit Christine. The visits went well, but somehow, my father found out about the last visit. How, I don't know. The threats became worse, threats against me and your parents, never against Christine. In his own twisted way, he must have loved her. His threats against Devin and your mother became more overt than in the past. I regret never warning them, but I assumed your parents always had protection."

"They did have some protection."

"I knew my father's threats were to be taken seriously. I simply stayed around, did nothing to anger my father, and waited. When he was found dead, we were released from any further threats. I have no clue what demons dogged my father all these years, but I have to admit that any love I had for him was spent long ago. When he died, I felt released from a dark and dank dungeon. My father was so self-centered he really had no love for anyone but himself and possibly for Christine. Women were playthings as far as he was concerned."

"Life must have been difficult for you."

"It was. I spent my life trying to protect and love my daughter. While I never warned your father, Lance, I did what I thought best. I'm so sorry."

"There's no reason to feel an apology necessary."

"Thank you. Over the years, especially after Christine reached the teenage years, I told her as much as I knew or had read about her father. She has her father's talent and looks and longs for an acting career in Hollywood. I'm grateful for you putting my mother and daughter in contact with Devin's agent. Helping her is appreciated."

"I'm pleased to do it, but I think you realize that Dad would want me to do that."

"Yes, I'm sure he would. He was a good man." At that moment, Val entered the room, and Anna rose. "Now, mother and I are going out so you and Christine can have some time together. She needs to know her brother. I'm delighted to meet and share all this with you. You seem to be a wonderful young man."

"Thank you." I stood and shook her extended hand.

As soon as Anna and Val had closed the door and entered the hall, Christine said, "You may wonder why my mother and grandmother left. They are meeting friends, but it's really because I requested time alone with my brother."

"We are brother and sister, yet we aren't brother and sister."

"What does that mean?"

"Mom and Dad couldn't have children for some reason. I was adopted when I was a few days old. I was their son in every way except genetically. We are not biologically related. I have a biological family out there I'm trying to find, but I'll be glad to have you as a sister, genetic connection or not. I'd like that very much."

"Thanks. I also grew up with no siblings. I like you, Little Brother." She smiled at me.

"Thanks."

"I feel a need to tell you about myself, Lance. Also, I very much want to hear about our father."

"Great."

"My mother has told me in great detail about her relationship with my father and what has happened since then. It's not a pleasant story or one I'd not wish on anyone. I don't recall meeting my father when I was five, but recall a bit about my visit with him when I was ten. I think Daddy and…. Daddy? You know, I think, that's what I called him the two times we were together. It's difficult to call him Daddy now because I've spent a lifetime without him, but saying Father doesn't seem right to me either. This brings tears to my eyes."

And indeed I noticed the tears. "Christine, you may call him Daddy, and it's okay to call him Father. Follow your heart."

"Lance, I think pictures were taken when I was with…" She paused briefly. "…when I was with Daddy and Erin if I recall correctly. Your mother's name was Erin, right?"

"You're correct on both points. The pictures are in two photo albums at home."

"I'd love to see them."

"And you will. You're welcome to come to the house. I know you have yet to be informed, but half of Dad's estate is yours."

"Mine?"

"Yes. It was in his will. It's only fair. All liquid assets are split 50-50 between us, but I was given the house in Malibu in which I grew up, while you were given the apartment house in Santa Monica. There's a lovely penthouse apartment atop that place.

You can see the Santa Monica pier and the ocean from the living room. You'll love it. You also have to meet with Rick, Dad's attorney. Now that I've found you, he can probate the will and settle everything."

"I'm overwhelmed by our father's generosity and also yours. I want to know more about our father."

"You will. But first, please finish your story for me."

"As you have been told, my grandmother divorced my grandfather years ago. It was messy. She fled to Italy and remained there. Mom chose to stay in New York so as not to anger my grandfather further. But our staying was not always pleasant. We moved to upstate New York and to Canada for brief periods. Why, I'm not sure. Grandfather had serial affairs, some of which were really scandalous, but his last was with the wrong woman. He ended on the wrong side of too many bullets. Even as a well-known attorney my grandfather was involved with some unsavory characters. His death was our freedom. Mother has already told you why she stayed all those years."

"Did he treat you well?"

"Better than my mother and grandmother were treated. I was aware of that as a youngster. I was granted a bit more freedom and was never threatened directly. I graduated from New York University with a theatre degree. Grandfather was fine with my attending that university, but I really wanted to enroll and study theatre at the University of Arizona. After my graduation, I began modeling. Grandmother's connections were helpful. Eventually, I defied my grandfather. That may have been around the time your mother died, I'm not certain. I left New York and modeled in Paris and Italy. That lead to two Italian film roles and finally to film roles in Australia. I have been working in Australian films for a number of years now.

"Why did you never come to Hollywood?"

"I often thought about doing that. I wanted to see…" She paused. "Daddy again, but I had this feeling that after all the years, I might be intruding and unwelcome."

"You would have been welcomed."

"I wish I had come to find him. In any case, my grandmother finally came to Los Angeles to arrange something for me through a friend. Then Daddy died, and she stayed on for the funeral service. There she met you, and through you I have contact with Daddy's agent."

"You knew Dad was a film star, didn't you?"

"Mother made that clear to me by the time I was a teenager. I saw as many of my father's films as possible. I was never to let my grandfather know I knew, and I guarded that secret. But mother always made it clear we could make no contact because of Daddy's safety. That was really difficult. When I learned the reason for no contact, I began to detest Grandfather. It's wrong to hate, yet it was so easy for me in my situation. I found it's much more difficult to forgive."

"Do you still hate him?"

"No, but overcoming my hatred for him was no easy task. A number of years ago, my mother met and later married a stage designer she met in New York. He was a Brit who at the time spent lots of time working in America designing sets for Broadway shows. Oddly enough, he was a devout Anglican. I think he was as much a boat sailing upstream in New York and London as Daddy was in Hollywood. It was through him that mother and I began attending church, and I eventually forgave Grandfather. I am not sure mother has fully done that yet, but she's trying. My forgiveness happened before Grandfather died. I was glad to restore some relationship. But it was sad to see Grandfather continue down the path leading to his destruction. Mother and my step-father now live in London where he works almost exclusively in the West End."

"London's Broadway, if I recall from our visits there. Right?

"Yes. He has been very successful, and he and mother are happy. She deserves the happiness that eluded her for so many years."

"So, what are your plans now?"

"I have spoken with Mr. Feldmann and will be going to Hollywood in two days for a screen test which he has arranged for me."

"Then, why not fly back to the coast with me and stay at the house. Dad's sister Alexa, your aunt, is visiting with me now. You simply have to meet her. And I'd love to have my sister meet my future wife, Alle. You'll like them both. In addition, I'd like to show you around Malibu, Hollywood, and Los Angeles. Plus, you have to check out your apartment house and the penthouse. I think the penthouse is vacant now, but Cliff could verify that."

"I'd love that, Lance."

"Christine, Dad left a letter for you."

"May I read it?"

"Tomorrow, I'll give it to you. You need to know Dad before you read his letter. What you have to do this evening is read Dad's journals. He wanted you to read them, then tomorrow morning I'll give you the letter. The journals are the best way to get acquainted with our dad, but I'll be happy to answer any questions you have after you've read them. When you stay at the house you also have to read my mom's diaries because they will fill in some blanks about Dad."

"Blanks?"

"The things which may not be clear from just reading Dad's journals."

I left Dad's journals with Christine and returned to The Plaza. My time with Val, Anna, and Christine kept playing in my head. Sleep was elusive until about 3:00 a.m. when I drifted into a deep sleep, only to be awakened about 8:00 a.m. with the phone ringing. I managed to pick it up after a few rings.

Chapter Eighteen

On the other end of the line was Christine asking if she could come to my room about nine-thirty. I rushed around, showered, shaved, dressed, grabbed a bite to eat downstairs, and was back in my room shortly before Christine arrived.

I opened the door after her knock to find a bleary-eyed Christine carrying Dad's journals and looking a bit as though she might have just left a mix-master. Her evening must have been difficult.

As she entered the room, she said, "I'm so sorry, I look like this, but I read all the journals and got very little sleep."

"I'll order coffee sent up." I ordered the coffee, turned to see her sitting on the sofa, and said, "I assume you have some thoughts after reading Dad's journals?"

The tears welled in her eyes as she replied to my question. "How I wish I had seen him after I was ten. He loved me, missed me, and even tried to find me. In a way, I'm glad I never knew that growing up, or my situation would have probably seemed even more painful and untenable. Never finding me and having no contact must have been painful for Daddy."

"I'm certain it was. Dad suffered in silence. I never had a clue. You know Dad was a religious man and obviously found solace in God and the beach. God, Mom, and the beach were his comforters. I think I now know the full meaning of the poem."

"What poem?"

"You have to read it yourself when we get to the coast tomorrow. It's about God lending children to us until he calls them home to be with Him. Dad must have in some way viewed you as a child lent to him but never allowed to stay. The poem always hung on their bedroom wall."

Christine looked at me and said, "Lance, so you never even suspected there was someone like me or that you were adopted, did you?"

"No, I never did. Mom's diaries and Dad's journals were also important to me. I learned so much about my parents that I never knew growing up. They were wonderful parents and loved deeply, not just me but others. You were deeply loved also, although only seen twice."

"That's so hard to fully understand, I suppose, if one does not personally experience it."

The knock on the door signaled room service delivering the coffee. After the attendant left, I poured our coffee, handing a cup to Christine as I said, "As 1st Corinthians 13 says, '…faith, hope, and love abide, these three; but the greatest of these is love.'"

"How I wish I could have known him growing up, perhaps I could have avoided so much pain in my own life."

"Christine, Dad's response to that would have been, 'Better to know now than never to have known.'"

"You are kind, Lance. I needed to hear that."

"Could I read my father's letter now?"

"Yes." I picked the letter off the table and handed it to her. "Now that you've read Dad's journals, I'm sure you will better appreciate what he says."

I watched Christine as she opened the envelope, removed Dad's letter, and began reading.

April 29, 1992

Dear Christine,

My wish would have been to tell you in person everything I share here. At age five and ten you were simply too young to hear what I have to say. And for reasons I never understood and still don't, I was never permitted to see you again. Only those two times! Know that I loved you then and love you still. I longed to see you, and often. You must be about 33 years old now. How I wish I had spent those years being your father.

I dated your mother from sometime in October until mid-December in 1958. Your mother was intelligent and very pretty. I did enjoy her company, but I have to be honest and say I never loved her, although I liked her a great deal. My interests were centered on a future career in acting. I think Anna was much more serious about me, whether it was love I don't know. On one occasion in early December 1958 we were intimate. I simply lost control, overcome with the passion of the moment. It was a violation of every religious and personal belief I hold. Afterward, I was overcome with remorse. Being a deeply religious person, I know God forgave me, but it took much longer for me to forgive myself. How your mother felt after that occurrence, I'm clueless.

In any case, on March 9, 1958, I arrived in the University of Arizona theatre lobby before my first class. The theatre department secretary handed me a letter from your mother. It read:

March 6, 1959

Dear Devin,

I wanted to let you know that I have quit school today. I'll be leaving my things with my grandparents at their condo to bring home for me in a few weeks. My flight back to New York leaves early in the morning.

You're a talented guy, and I enjoyed knowing you and our time together. I'm sad it didn't work out with us, but you've left me with a wonderful gift. Someday, I'll thank you in person for it. I hope you can remember me pleasantly from time to time. It was never my intention to hurt you, but I was certain I loved you and hoped there'd be a future for us. It wasn't to be I guess. No, I'm not angry, just a bit hurt and confused, but I'll be fine once I'm home.

Enjoy your career. I know how important that is to you. I wish you success, but I'm confident that with your talent, your dreams will be realized. I'll know because you'll be famous. I'm confident of that.

Please make no effort to contact me in the future. If you do, you'll not find me. My father will see to that. At some point in the future, I'll contact you. Please allow me my own time and space to do that when I'm ready. I need the space now. Be assured, I will contact you. Until then, I'll think about you often. Take care.

My love,

Anna

I didn't understand what Anna meant by "left me a wonderful gift," but a child did occur to me. After meeting with my pastor, I chose to respect your mother's wishes. Was I right? I'm not sure.

When you were five, your mother contacted me and arranged for me to meet you at the top of the Empire State Building. From the moment I knew of your existence, I regretted not trying to find Anna in 1959. But having looked for her and you since then, I have no doubt my hunt would have been unfruitful. Your mother contacted me again when you were ten. We met you that time also atop the Empire State Building. You probably have no recollection of that first visit, but perhaps you recall some of the second one. Did I want to see you more often? Yes, I did. I was always willing, but I never had a telephone number or an address. In fact, I never knew what name you and your mother were using. Why I didn't see you often is something only your mother can explain to you. Believe me when I tell you that I wanted to see you. I was only permitted to see you when your mother contacted me. I've been trying to find you for years, but was never successful.

My son Lance is adopted, and his mother and I loved him from the first moment we saw him. He doesn't know his adoption status or about you as I write this letter; he will know though by the time he locates you. As parents we were derelict in never telling him. I regret that now. Lance is a wonderful young man, and I am sure you will enjoy knowing him. My sister Alexa, your aunt also, is his only close relative, unless and until he locates his biological family. I'm sure he would enjoy a sister relationship, Christine, if you find that possible.

If Lance somehow, someday manages to locate you and deliver this letter, I'd like to look down on the two of you, but doubt that ability is a part of heaven. You see, I am in my final weeks of life. Cancer! God has given me a wonderful life, a wife I loved with all my heart who was killed in an auto accident four years ago, and a son who was the joy of our lives. Having had you as a part of our family would have provided all of us additional joy, especially me.

I missed you not being a part of my life, our life. I missed providing for you as a father should. I missed teaching you religious and personal values. I missed witnessing your education. I missed hearing about your interests. I missed watching you in your activities. But most of all, I missed being your father, holding you when you were hurt, kissing those hurts away, hugging you and having you hug me, telling you I love you and hearing you return those words, saying a bedtime prayer with you each night, and kissing you goodnight. I would like to hold you now and tell you, "I love you." I'd love to take another walk with you in Central Park as we did when you were five and ten. I'd love to enjoy ice cream with you again. I'd love to attend another Broadway show with you as we did so long ago. Since none of that will ever be again, always remember I loved you then, and love you now.

Since I was unable to provide for you before and after you were born, I'll provide for you now and into the future. While you may not need it; just know I get much joy in providing for you finally that which I have been unable to do before. Lance will explain all this to you.

As I end this, know I love you. Since we will not meet again in this life, it is my prayer we will meet again in the next. I'll look forward to that.

May God bless and richly reward you.

My love,
Your father

By the time Christine had finished reading the letter, she was sobbing. I moved to the sofa and held her as she cried. I heard her brokenly say almost to herself, "This was my Daddy…I want to talk with him…He loved me…He really did love me."

When she calmed, I said, "Yes, he really loved you. He loved both of us. Dad loved easily and was easy to love."

Finally, after a long pause, she calmed and said, "So where do we go from here, Lance?"

"Tomorrow morning we fly to the coast. You meet Billy Feld-mann, have your screen test, and then I suspect a new life and a film career await you. The darkness and shadows are breaking, the morning is dawning, and your dream will take flight."

Chapter Nineteen

Christine and I flew to Los Angeles the next morning. After landing and getting our baggage, we got into my car where I'd parked when Val and I had flown east, and headed for Malibu and home.

After leaving the airport, we headed north on the 405 freeway, then west on the 10 freeway into Santa Monica. Once we left Santa Monica, we travelled on the Pacific Coast Highway. Having never been in California before, Christine was intrigued by the views.

When we arrived at the house and had put her bags in a guest room, we had coffee in the kitchen with Alex, and all of us walked down to the beach. Alex and Christine seemed to enjoy each other.

The next morning, I drove her to Billy's office and made the introduction. We all got into Billy's car and drove over to Crossroad Studios for Christine's screen test. Once that was concluded, Billy took us to the commissary for lunch. Billy introduced us to everyone he knew, and he knew almost everyone. Christine told me later she was a bit overwhelmed, even though she'd been around Italian and Australian movie studios for a number of years. When Billy let us off at my car, he told Christine he would be in touch in the next few days.

*****

One evening three weeks after my letters had been mailed to the adoption agency, the phone rang. I answered.

"Bradshaw residence," I said.

"I'm calling to speak with Lance Bradshaw."

"This is Lance speaking."

"Mr. Bradshaw, I'm Tom Preston, with Center for Hope in Seattle. I'm calling to tell you we received your letter, were able to contact your birth mother, and forwarded your letter to her."

"You've spoken with her?"

"Yes, earlier this afternoon as a matter of fact."

My heart raced. My mind became an instant jumble of thoughts. What could I say? A few seconds and some deep breaths restored me to some normality. Finally, I said, "Was she unhappy about the contact?"

"She was shocked to hear from us after all these years, but was thrilled that you desired contact. I'm not at liberty to give you her personal information now, but she said to tell you when she receives your letter, she'll be in contact. I hope that is okay."

"Of course. Have you made contact with my birth father also?"

"Unfortunately, we haven't. There's nothing in our records that would enable us to contact him. We have no information on him except the information given your parents at the time of your adoption. Your birth mother will have to provide his name."

"Thank you, Mr. Preston."

"We're glad to have been of assistance. Do you have any other questions, Mr. Bradshaw?"

"No. I look forward to hearing from her. I appreciate all you've done. Thanks."

"You're welcome. If you need anything further, please feel free to write or call. Have a good evening."

Have a good evening? You have to be kidding me. How can I have a good evening? Not this one or any in the future until that letter arrives.

I turned after putting down the phone to find Aunt Alex and Christine standing in the doorway staring at me. "Well," Alex said, "that must have been good news?"

"It was," I replied. "That was the Seattle adoption agency. They've made contact with my birth mother, forwarded my letter to her, and she'll be writing soon."

"That's terrific, Lance. Now I'm sure you have a number of rather restless nights facing you."

"You know, Aunt Alex, I was just thinking the same thing when I saw you standing there."

Yeah, the night was restless, as were a few others following. I spent my days walking along the beach, swimming, playing the piano, or just sitting on the patio looking out at the ocean. I was never very good at waiting but was glad to have both Alex and Christine around to distract me. I never waited patiently for Christmas or much of anything else. Instant gratification wasn't my forte either; I had been taught better than that. Some waits were worth the time, maybe my wait for this anticipated letter would be one of those. I kept hoping.

Days later, the letter appeared in the mail box. I called Aunt Alex and Christine to come to the kitchen while I read it.

July 26, 1992

Dear Lance,

For years I've thought about having to write this letter if the occasion ever arose. Even though I had thought about it all these years, it's been difficult for me to write this, explaining why it has taken me so long.

Your letter and the pictures arrived. Thank you so much. What a joy to see such a handsome young man, my son, looking back at me in those pictures. It was the impossible dream which came true.

I looked up at Alex and Christine and said, "You know I finally fully understand why Mom and Dad, especially Dad, loved 'The Impossible Dream,' lyrics and music." They both smiled, even though they had no clue what I'd just read. I returned to reading.

It did come as a shock to read your father was Devin MacArthur. I always enjoyed his movies. I'd read about his death, but couldn't recall much in the newspapers or magazines about him or his family over the years. He must have jealously guarded his and the family's privacy. You benefited, I'm sure. I'm so sorry to hear you have lost both your parents. I know from personal experience how difficult that is, having lost both my parents, your biological grandparents, in the last ten years. But you're a young man, and your loss must be more difficult than mine.

Over the years, I often wondered about you—what you looked like, how your life was going, if you ever thought of me. I want you to know that you were never forgotten and were always loved.

I'm not sure where to begin, what you might want to know, but I'll share what I think you may want to know now. I'll be happy to answer any additional questions you may have later.

I was in my early 20's when you were born. I was a secretary, having completed a two-year program at a local community college. I worked in an office down the hall from your birth father's office. He was a few years older than I and an executive engineer with the aeronautical firm. We'd been seeing one other for a little over a year when I became pregnant. When I told him about the pregnancy, he told me he was married but had been going through marital problems. I never knew about any separation from his wife nor did I ever suspect he was a married man. He had nothing to do with me after I became pregnant, and returned to his wife as far as I know. I heard later that he and his wife had a child. I've not seen or heard from him since.

I had no family support during my pregnancy, but a supportive friend told me about this Seattle agency that helped young women in my situation. Even though I had health insurance through work, the agency provided additional services to me. Yes, I considered an abortion, but rejected it. I simply couldn't do that to the life growing inside me. My child deserved a stable family and a home with lots of love. I could have provided the love, but little else at the time. That's why I made an adoption plan for you. It was difficult to give up my child, the child that I'd carried for nine months and loved, but I knew you deserved a chance at a life better than I could provide. I always feared you would hate me. And during all these years, every little blond, blue-eyed boy I saw brought a tear to my eyes and the nagging thought, "Could that be my little boy?" I cannot describe the pain of giving up a child you love, so they could have a chance at a better life. I just hope and pray that you can understand and accept my reasoning.

Having recently seen a production of <u>Miss Saigon</u>, I felt I had an elementary understanding of the pain and suffering a mother might have experienced giving up a child.

I moved on with building a life as best I could. I've had a good life, but you've always been in my heart and had my love. I always hoped and prayed that you would someday search for me. I'm not certain I would have ever searched for you, even though I wanted to do that many times. I simply thought and was told by a number of people, rightly or wrongly, I didn't have the right to interfere with your life.

Your birth father was over six feet tall, about 180 pounds, slender, and had an athletic build.

I'd share more but am unsure what else you might want to know at this time.

I'd love to hear about you, your life, your plans and goals, but most of all I hope you can accept and understand why I surrendered you for adoption.

If you're willing to meet with me, I'm willing to do that, either in Los Angeles or here in Seattle, your choice. However, if you'd prefer to only exchange letters for now, that's also fine. Whatever you would find most comfortable, I'll support and respect.

Please remember you have never been forgotten. I've always loved you, then and now.

I'm listed in the phone directory so obtaining my number should not be difficult.

With much love,
Your birth mother, Elsa Rae Barrett

Tears were rolling down my cheeks as I finished the letter and handed it to Aunt Alex to read. When she finished, she handed it to Christine and looked at me, tears in her eyes also, and said, "Well?"

"What can I say, Alex? I want to meet her. The situation she faced with no support couldn't have been easy. I understand that much. I want to talk with her. She may be that unexplainable something I've always felt was missing in my life. What do you think?"

"Perhaps she is. I think you should contact her, Lance, the sooner the better. You should have no difficulty getting her phone number. Do it when you feel the time is right."

"Lance, I'd do it now," said Christine looking up from her reading of the letter. "Waiting didn't help me or Daddy. The right time is now."

"The right time is probably tonight. I need to reflect on all this and decide what to say. So after dinner I'll go into the study, get her number from directory assistance, and make the call. Now, I think I need a walk on the beach to release some tension. Would you two like to join me?"

"I will as soon as I finish reading this," said Christine, looking at Alex who nodded yes.

Alex said, "Let's go in a few minutes then. We might all be able to unwind and relax out there."

Walking along the beach and conversing helped to release some of my tension. I felt lighter, no longer carrying the heavy weight of anticipation.

That evening, I did call Elsa. I hadn't really planned what to say but decided I'd just wing it. She answered on the first ring. "Hello."

"Hi, this is Lance."

"Oh, my…" I began to think she might have fainted. Finally, she said, "I'd wondered if you'd received my letter."

"I did, just today. Thanks so much for writing. It means a lot."

"Well, you were overdue an explanation. I'm glad to have contact. Thanks so much for calling me. You don't know how much. I love the letter and the pictures. You're such a handsome young man."

"Thanks." I paused wondering what to say next. Finally, a thought came to me. "I'd like you to come down to LA if you can and want to do that."

"I can, and I'd like to. When?"

"As soon as possible. How about this weekend? Come on Friday. We can visit over the weekend."

"I'll make reservations tomorrow."

"Great. Call me when you have them. I'll meet you at LAX."

"I'll call back as soon as I have an arrival time and flight number."

"And I'll make your hotel reservations, so we can be close."

"Oh, I can do that, Lance."

"Please, I insist."

"Okay, if you want to take care of it."

"By the way, you've seen my pictures, so you know what I look like. I have no clue about you though, so I'll just wait for the beautiful, older 'cougar' to pick me out of the crowd and carry me away." I heard her laugh.

"Now, aren't you the funny one. I'll call tomorrow. Okay?"

"I'll be waiting. It's wonderful to finally talk with you."

"Yes, it is. I'm so glad you called."

I had no intention of making hotel reservations, but instead would bring her to the house in Malibu. I knew I'd feel more comfortable in familiar surroundings. She on the other hand, would be in unfamiliar territory regardless of where she stayed. I wanted her to see where I'd grown up and to meet my family.

Chapter Twenty

July 1992

Christine's screen test had gone well. The studio signed her to a contract and gave her a new name, Christine MacArthur. According to Billy, the intent was to publicize the fact she was Dad's daughter. Christine's waiting game began, a wait for the right property to utilize her beauty and talent and to showcase her to the public.

On the day Elsa arrived, I reached LAX early, checked the arrival monitor, and positioned myself near the gate for her flight. I periodically rechecked the monitor and had to move to two other gates before the flight finally came.

I was confident Elsa would recognize me from all the pictures I'd sent her, but I, on the other hand, had no clue what she looked like. As passengers began to enter the gate area, I'd just have to wait. I'd told Alle, Aunt Alex, and Christine about the cougar comment I'd made to Elsa on the phone. After joking with Alle that I'd create a "Cougar Prey" sign to hold up so Elsa would quickly spot me, she just laughed and retorted, "That sounds a bit like the stunt with the Elizabeth Barrett Browning book your Dad staged for your mother in order to gain her attention." Of course, I still thought the sign a rather clever idea.

I positioned myself apart from the crowd gathered at the gate awaiting the incoming Seattle flight. A few minutes later, passengers began emerging. Would she see me? At first, all the passengers moved along to the baggage area, but then I saw this attractive, stylishly-dressed woman enter who appeared to search the crowd for a face. My "cougar" no doubt! Quickly, she focused on me and walked my direction.

Suddenly, she was in front of me. Being unsure what to do, I extended my hand and said, "I'm Lance. You must be Elsa."

She took my hand in both of hers and began to weep. I immediately took her into my arms as she continued weeping. I didn't know what else to do. Handling crying women wasn't an experience I'd previously had.

Slowly, she pulled back, looked at me, and said, "I never saw you after you were born and have dreamed of seeing you for over 20 years." She touched my cheeks. "I just want to touch you. I don't want to embarrass you, but may I hold you? When you were born I was not allowed to hold you."

I responded, "Yes." She held me in a warm embrace and cried. I experienced a strange sensation during her embrace, a warmth, and an unexplainable feeling the something missing in my life clicked into place. That would take some thought to fully comprehend.

Eventually, I said, "Elsa, let's get your bag. We can talk in the car. She took my hand as we walked toward the baggage claim carousel. She indicated her bag as it neared us. I grabbed it before it passed. As we began walking toward my parked car, she again took my hand. Periodically, I noticed she would glance at me and smile, a satisfied smile.

When we reached the car, she said, "A Mustang? You drive a Mustang?"

"Yes. They seem to run in the family. Dad drove one. My grandfather owned a Ford dealership. There's some genetic link, I think." Elsa smiled.

"I was worried when I read in your letter that your father was Devin MacArthur."

"Elsa, you needn't have worried. My parents had wealth and fame, but it never went to their heads. Dad always said, 'Fame is fleeting; it's just wind.' They were simply normal and loving people in spite of money and fame."

"I'm so glad you had such a family."

I put her bag in the car, we both got in, and I headed out of the airport toward the San Diego Freeway. As I drove north toward Santa Monica, I pointed out various spots and landmarks, and we made small talk, nothing of substance. In Santa Monica, we got on the Pacific Coast Highway. Elsa turned to me and said, "Where's my hotel?"

"Well, it's like this, Elsa. You're staying at our house in Malibu. My Aunt Alex, Dad's sister, and my sister Christine are staying with me; plus Mona, our cook and housekeeper, is there during the day."

"Lance, I don't want to impose."

"No imposition at all. I want you to stay where I grew up. We want you to stay there."

"You're sure?"

"I'm certain. Don't worry. You're safe with all of us, and I can assure you there are no Hollywood bad guys around."

When we arrived home, I took her bag, placed it by the front stairs, and led her into the kitchen where Mona had a cup of coffee for each of us. Following coffee, I asked Elsa if she wanted to go to her room and change into something more comfortable; then we could walk on the beach.

"Yes, that'd be great," she said. "I need to stretch my legs anyway. Let me change and put on another pair of shoes."

I picked up her bag, led her upstairs to her room, and told her I'd be on the patio when she was ready. I grabbed another cup of coffee before I went out to the patio. Now, I had met my birth mother. Strange feelings and thoughts I have. I do feel comfortable with her. Is that genetic? Some would call her a beautiful blonde. She's definitely attractive, engaging, and warm; yet she's not Mom. Hopefully, another kind of relationship will develop. What kind? I wondered. Thirty or so minutes later, she came out in a becoming, casual pants suit. I had begun to wonder what had happened to her.

"Lance, the house is lovely. I met Alexa and Christine, and they gave me the grand tour. I enjoyed seeing all the family photos."

"I'm glad you have met them. It's a comfortable house. Since Dad died, it doesn't seem much like home anymore."

"Of course it's your home," Elsa replied. "You're still in the grief process. It'll seem like home again soon, I'm certain."

"Well, if you're ready, let me show you around the property. Then, we'll go down and walk on the beach."

*****

As we walked along the beach later, waves rolling in and a cool ocean breeze blowing, Elsa said, "Lance, I'd love to hear about you."

I smiled. "Well, I was born in…"

"I think I know all about that, Lance." She smiled sadly.

"As I understand it Mom and Dad were at the hospital in Renton when I was born."

"I didn't know that. So they saw you right after you were born?"

"Yes. Dad and Mom always told me about holding me the first time. And when I was released from the hospital, we flew back home."

"So, you've always lived here?"

"Yes. It's the only home I've known. I love being close to the ocean. It's beautiful here and relaxing."

"Yes, it is. Where'd you go to school?"

"Mom and Dad were not happy with my kindergarten program, so they put me in a Catholic elementary school at the beginning of my first grade."

"Were they Catholic? Not that it matters. I'm just curious."

"We belonged to a large non-denominational church in Santa Monica. Always have. Dad's lawyer recommended the school because his son attended. Mom and Dad were impressed with the school principal, Sister Margaret. At their first meeting with Sister Margaret, they asked her what discipline was like in her school. She had responded, 'When a child gets in trouble, we paddle if parents have approved our paddling. If not, we use alternative discipline measures. Then we call the parents, and we do it in that order.' Both Mom and Dad had responded, 'We like that. Enroll him.' My parents liked her firmness; they always seemed to enjoy telling the story. I think Mom and Dad always kept me in Catholic schools, even through high school, to shield me."

"Shield you from what…publicity?"

"Yeah, from publicity, I think. And I was always Bradshaw, not MacArthur. That also made publicity less likely. I went to Saint Paul's High School, a boy's high school."

"Was that difficult for you?"

"Not really. There was a Catholic girl's high school not far away. The two schools combined play productions and dances. There were plenty of girls."

"It's good to hear that you didn't waste your high school years in a monastery."

"Oh, I didn't. There were also plenty of girls at the University of Arizona where I got my BA." Elsa chuckled. "That was also Mom and Dad's alma mater."

"Bet they wanted you to go there."

"Yes, that's where they always wanted me to go, but once I'd visited the campus a few times, attending was my goal, not just theirs."

"What sort of interests did you have in school?"

"I always had piano lessons, and…"

"Do you play well?"

"Not bad. Mom…"

"You'll have to play for me while I'm here."

"I'll do that. Mom and Dad both played the piano. We always had a great time playing and singing around the piano, especially at Christmas, but also at other times."

"Did you play sports?"

"I was a swimmer in the early grades. Always ran track and was good at that. I have a few trophies in my room that I can show you. And I also played tennis. Although I liked tennis, I was much better at track."

"No baseball, basketball, or football?"

"My parents didn't want me involved in those contact sports. I had a head injury in the summer between my first and second grades. Ran in front of a car. It really scared Mom and Dad, but I made a complete recovery. Mom and Dad always said it was God's second gift to them."

"And what was the first?"

"Me. Anyway, because of the head injury, they didn't want me involved in any sport like basketball or football."

"But baseball isn't a contact sport?"

"No, but Dad always told me, 'That little baseball is hard.' So I didn't play that either. But you know, I didn't resist too much. Well, Mom thought I did. Early on, I discovered I really enjoyed swimming, and in high school I truly loved tennis and track. Plus, I was involved in high school theatre. I stayed plenty busy."

"What's your BA in?"

"Theatre, of course, but I also have a teaching certificate. Acting was okay, but I always preferred directing and backstage work."

"Do, you plan to teach?"

"Yes, on the college level. But I need a master's degree for that, so it's back to the University of Arizona next year. Now, Elsa, I want to hear about you." We sat down on a large rock.

"Where do you want me to begin?"

"Anywhere you want."

"I always intended a happy life. However, there was never the happiness I intended, but it wasn't unhappy. Giving you up for adoption was my dark shadow. That brought years of pain for me and my family. Don't think I'm blaming you. The situation I found myself in and what I did about it caused the pain, but I saw no other solution at the time." I noticed she had tears in her eyes.

"My parents never told me I was adopted. I found out after Dad died. My shock, I think, was how and when I found out I was adopted, not really so much that I was adopted. I'm sure abortion was an option. I'm glad you chose to give me life."

"I regret you weren't told when you were young. You would probably have found that easier. I must admit I considered an abortion. I even went in for one, but left quickly. I really had no choice. I had to give you a chance at life. I regret, though, we have lost so much time."

"Thank you for a second chance at life. It turned out just fine for me. I had a family who loved me. We can make up some of what we've lost."

"I hope so. There were three of us in my family. Oh, I had a brother, Peter, who passed away when he was young, from a heart problem. His death contributed to problems between my parents. There was never the same happiness in our home after Pete died. My mother was a secretary for a business executive, and my father, a math teacher. My parents were strict. I was like most kids, I guess, in wanting to get out of the house and have more independence. My parents' goal for my life included a four-year college education and marriage to a respectable man. As soon as I graduated from high school, I enrolled at a local community college where I received an associate degree. I followed a secretarial and business-related program. Upon receiving my degree, I accepted a position as an executive secretary with an aeronautical firm. It was there that I met Hunter Brett Cameron. He was tall, dark, and handsome, and he had an easy-going, engaging personality, much like my father's in many ways. Our relationship developed over many months and became serious. "

"Hunter Brett Cameron. Now that's a name for you. It sounds so Hollywoodish," I muttered half to myself. I noticed Elsa looked at me with a sad smile.

"I'd rented an apartment when I got my job so I'd have independence. Brett, as I called him, was more than willing to come to my apartment. I think he had a small apartment in Bellevue, but after what happened in our relationship, I'm not certain. Looking back on our year together, there was always a hidden part of Brett's life, at least hidden from me. Why I failed to see it at the time, I never understood. My parents seemed to sense something was amiss which may explain why they weren't supportive when I became pregnant."

"What was he like, Elsa?"

"Brett was a wonderful man, I thought. I fell in love. Our relationship was kept a secret at work, only pursued after work hours. He was kind and good to me. He liked to joke, laugh, watch movies, and play tennis. Everyone liked him."

"What happened when I came along?"

"About a year or so into our relationship, I became pregnant. When I told Brett, he said he could never marry me because he was already married and had been separated. I never knew or even suspected. Shows how naïve I was. He was soon transferred to a position at another of the firm's locations in the area, probably at his request. I never saw him again." Elsa was dabbing the tears in her eyes.

"Did you talk to him after I was born?"

"I managed to get his new office phone number, called him shortly after you were born and told him that I'd placed you for adoption. He said that was best and thanked me rather curtly for calling."

"And you never married?"

"No. I'm not sure why I didn't. Oh, I dated, off and on, but there was never another man who captured my attention and certainly none I cared deeply about. To marry just to marry without loving deeply seemed foolish to me. It still does. So, I never married. That's the only reason I can give you."

"Do you regret that?"

"Sometimes I do, especially when I'm lonely, but I've had a good life, fulfilling, active, and certainly not unhappy - happier than I ever thought possible shortly after you were born and surrendered. From the moment Brett left, I was angry. That anger festered for many months. I lashed out at everyone, but eventually I had to tell them my condition. A few close friends became my support group; unfortunately, my parents weren't among them. I was an embarrassment. It'd be years before our relationship was repaired. Both my parents developed health issues requiring my assistance, and our relationship was finally reestablished. They weren't there when I needed them most, but I felt compelled to be there when they needed me most. I had to honor my parents."

"Elsa, let's go in now. After dinner we can talk more in the study, if that's okay."

"That's fine. Talking about this part of my life is emotionally draining."

"I'm sorry."

"Don't be sorry about it. You've a right to know, and I have a need to share. A break, though, will do us both good."

*****

After dinner, Mona cleaned the kitchen and walked home. Alex and Christine went to their bedrooms, while Elsa and I went into the study. As we sat, she said, "You know, I'm so thankful you had a good life and wonderful parents. I also really like Alexa and Christine. I never knew you had a sister."

"Well, I didn't grow up with an older sister. She was a daughter Dad didn't know he had until she was five. He only saw her twice."

"That's sad."

"Yes, it is. I'll tell you about it another time. Now back to your story."

"All I was ever told by the adoption agency was that you 'went to a loving family.' They did tell me you had blue eyes and blond hair but only after I asked."

"What were you told about my adoption?"

"Only that you went to a loving family where you fit in nicely. Not very comforting."

"I'm sure it wasn't."

"I had so many questions. Who are these people? What are they like? What kind of home do they provide my son? The questions never stopped. In addition, I was told by others that once I'd placed you for adoption the experience would be over, and I could get on with my life. For me, the reality was far different. The ordeal was never over."

"Elsa, I'm sorry you worried about me."

"It was best that you never had to worry, Lance. I spent years wondering where my baby was. Was he healthy? Was he happy? Was he loved? Was he alive? Every little blond, blue-eyed child I saw could be my baby! Every time I read about a child dying, I was sure it was my baby. Every kid in trouble, on drugs, on alcohol, was my baby. Every little waif I saw on the streets in Seattle was my baby. Does my child need me? Does my child ever think of me? Would I ever see him again? The questions were endless and painful. I wanted to see you again, but I had also been told my boy would have a new life, and I should never intrude. If I did that, he would be harmed."

"But I was fine the whole time."

"If I'd only known you were fine, it would have helped. My needs and my feelings were supposed to have died when I signed those surrender papers. They didn't. Had my feelings died, it would have been helpful. The pain of not knowing, of wondering, year after year, became almost unbearable at times. In order to endure the pain I had to shut my feelings out. In doing so a part of me died. But my love and longing for my baby never left me. That was what was so terrible about going on."

"Did you ever want to look for me?"

"There were times when I wanted to locate you, but I never convinced myself that my own pain could justify intruding on your life and possibly causing you pain or harm. So those moments were always suppressed."

"How did you feel when you were told I was looking for you?"

"I was shocked to receive the call from the Center for Hope saying you wanted contact, yet I was thrilled. I decided to write you a letter. It was difficult; I didn't know what to say. Even though I'd thought about having to do that someday, I still didn't know exactly what to say. Shortly before finishing my letter to you, I received your letter with the pictures. I was overwhelmed. After years of wondering what my son looked like, I had pictures of you as a baby through your high school graduation. How handsome you were. You still are. I could see a personal resemblance, but I felt you looked like your birth father, only you were fair, had blue eyes and blond hair, whereas he was dark. The first time I talked with you on the phone I was blown away. The emotional release for me after all these years was helpful. I finally felt some peace. I cried during almost the entire call and used lots of Kleenex. You may not have known I was crying."

"I thought maybe you were, but I wasn't sure."

"Lance, unfortunately, I can't erase our past. I can't relive my life as I'd ideally have liked it to have been. I can only look to the future. In many ways, I'm not the person I was in 1970. I know I can never fully recover what I lost when I placed you for adoption, regardless of what relationship we have in the future. But it's important to me to have a relationship."

"It is for me also, especially now." I paused, not sure what else to say.

"I'm emotionally drained and need an evening's rest. Is that okay?"

"Yes. I'm a bit drained myself."

"Thanks so much, Lance. I feel better than I have in years about all this. It's wonderful to finally be able to meet you and share my story."

"Thank you for answering the questions that have been running through my mind since reading Dad's letter. I'll see you in the morning. Would you enjoy seeing some of the area tomorrow?"

"I'd love that. There's so much that I've never seen in the LA area, I'm sure. Goodnight and thanks."

She went on up to her room. I went to my room a short time later. Although tired, I felt somewhat like a little kid finding his first Easter egg—immense joy. Also, I no longer had that old nagging feeling that a part of me was missing.

While I intended to crawl into bed and sleep, the emotional high overwhelmed me. I simply had to share all I'd experienced with Alle.

She answered quickly. "Hi, Lance. How did it go?"

"You remember my telling you once I always felt a part of me was missing?"

"Yeah, I do. I've often thought about that feeling. I just finished reading a book called The Primal Wound: Understanding the Adopted Child which offers some insight on that very topic."

"What point does it make?"

"Basically, the point is that separation from the birth mother has many effects on adopted children. One being the bond with the birth mother is broken."

"I've got to read that book, but I also had the strangest feeling when Elsa embraced me."

"What did you experience?"

"I felt she was the part of me which I always thought had been missing. Could that be?"

"Lance, based on the book I just read, that is probably what you experienced. Be grateful the missing part has returned."

"Oh, I am. The other strange thing is that I not once had any feeling I would be rejected."

"I'm so happy for you. For some reason, there have been times since I've known you when I wondered if there wasn't something you feared. Did you ever fear I'd reject you at some point?"

"Alle, while you never gave me any reason to feel that, I have to be honest and say the thought hit me a few times."

"Rejection was also a point in the book."

"Perhaps that feeling is now behind us."

"Hopefully. Thanks for being supportive, now and in the past. I love you."

"Love you too. So how do you feel after meeting Elsa?"

"A bit strange. Somewhat surreal. My feet are not touching the ground yet; it's as though I'm floating. Awesome and extremely happy. You have to meet her. Could you fly out?"

"Yes, and I'd love to. I miss you."

"Make your reservations, call me, and I'll meet you at LAX."

"I'll do that as soon as I hang up. I'll see you tomorrow."

"Looking forward to seeing you and your meeting my missing piece. Love you."

"Love you too. See you tomorrow."

Elsa stayed longer than the weekend. We changed her return flight, so she had a few days into the next week with us. Alle did arrive the next morning and spent a few days with us. What a relief to have the assurance Alle and Elsa enjoyed each other's company. Christine and Alle had only met once, and I was delighted they would have more time to become better acquainted.

During the remaining time Elsa spent with me, we saw many of the typical tourist spots in the area, and toured Dad's studio, arranged by Billy. Alex, Christine, and Alle took Elsa shopping in Hollywood, on Rodeo Drive, and showed her Dad's star on the Walk of Fame. We found we all enjoyed each other's company. At the end of her visit, Elsa was no longer just my birth mother; she was a friend. When I kissed her goodbye, she invited me to visit her in Seattle. I accepted.

Chapter Twenty-one

Fall 1992

For many weeks after Elsa told me the name of my birth father, I mentally debated attempting to locate him. I had formed a negative image of him, whether justified or not, after hearing Elsa's story. Was he basically a good man, yet flawed as are we all, or was his behavior nefarious? I had no conclusive way of discerning.

Following many discussions with Aunt Alex, Christine, and Alle, I finally concluded that I had to make an effort to contact him, simply for my own information. I needed to know my full background.

Through his professional engineer's association, I located his work address. I preferred not sending a letter to his home address because I desired to respect his privacy. I suppose also in the back of my mind was the thought that he might more likely have a positive reception to my letter if I didn't use his home address. I spent days writing and rewriting before I had a final copy of the letter I mailed him.

October 3, 1992

Dear Mr. Cameron:

This correspondence has been sent to your office in order to prevent any problem for you with your family. Enclosed you will find a number of personal photographs.

I've been told my birth father's name was Hunter Brett Cameron, an aeronautical engineer, who lived in Bellevue, Washington, at the time of my birth. My careful search led me to you. This is my sincere effort to respect your privacy. While I have no desire to intrude, embarrass, or cause hurt to you and/or your family, I have a need and a right to know my background. I'm not responsible for the circumstances of my birth, but I did and do have to live with them.

The desire for information about one's own roots is a universal need. Much has been written about this phenomenon. It is my desire to gain the final pieces of information necessary for me to have a complete background picture.

The basic facts of my birth are these:

> Mother: Elsa Rae Barrett
>
> Date of Birth: September 5, 1970
>
> Place of Birth: Renton, Washington
>
> Name given me at birth: Brett Ray Barrett

In addition to my birth father's name, Elsa gave me the following information: She and my birth father met at work and started seeing each other. My birth father, she later discovered, was married. He was over six feet tall, had brown hair, brown eyes, and weighed about 180 pounds. She said she hasn't seen or heard from him since before my birth, but she did inform him of my birth.

I would like my "adopted state" behind me. In order to do that, I need information. I pray you will assist me in putting this matter to rest. You must understand that I seek nothing from you, but I would like contact. I'd also find it helpful to have information regarding the following:

1. Has any birth family member had health issues that may be genetic?

2. Do I have any half-siblings?

3. What are the educational backgrounds of family members

4. Other than yourself, was anyone in your family aware of my birth?

5. What are the nationality backgrounds and occupations of your parents and grandparents for a genealogical record?

Sincerely,
Lance Evan Bradshaw

Enclosures: Personal photographs

I'd concluded after what Elsa had said about my birth father that my letter might not be welcomed. Maybe he didn't care. Maybe he didn't want this interruption in his life. Perhaps he didn't want his past indiscretion known by his family. Possibly all those positions had some justification, especially to him, but I felt differently. I thought I was owed full information on my past. While I didn't think I had any right to a relationship, I thought I was owed one personal meeting. Is it wrong to feel that way? Is it wrong to want to meet your father?

I moved on with plans for graduate school. The ranch near Redding Dad had asked Cliff to sell finally closed, and my share of the money was invested. Christine and I decided to sell the house in Tucson when I finished graduate school.

Christine had finally been cast in a movie which was currently filming. She had also left us and moved into the penthouse atop her apartment building in Santa Monica. She was enjoying life in California, but we saw her often. We also see Anna and Val when they come to visit Christine.

Weeks passed without any response to my letter. Finally, on December 15, I received the long-awaited response.

December 11, 1992

Lance,

I'm sure this correspondence isn't what you were seeking when you wrote me, but it'll have to do.

The past has a way of catching up with us, doesn't it? That's obviously true in my case. I'm not proud of what happened years ago, but it's now behind me, and I want to leave it there. I did wonder periodically what happened to Elsa's baby.

I allowed a few problems to lead me astray. Don't let that happen to you.

I'd prefer to see my life continue as it is currently and would like no further contact. You seem to have had the parents you needed.

The answers to your genealogical and health questions follow:

1. High blood pressure is the only family health issue.

2. Prefer not to respond regarding any half siblings.

3. I have a degree in aeronautical engineering. My parents both had college degrees.

4. I was the only one who knew about you.

5. My father's family is Italian; my mother's is French. My grandparents on both sides died before my birth. I never knew them.

Good luck living the rest of your life, and may God bless you in everything.

Hunter Cameron

Talk about killing my Christmas spirit. This almost did it for me. My anger, justified or not, had slowly risen as I'd read his letter. It was a brush-off. Intellectually, I knew he owed me nothing, but emotionally I felt differently. I had expected a response more empathetic; this was unkind, I thought. I know human beings are complex with sometimes seemingly contrasting aspects to their personalities. What kind of man was he? Was he really someone I wanted to meet and know? How could the Elsa I knew have loved this person? I had no answers. It was all perplexing. For him to have used the term "Elsa's baby" told me he assumed no responsibility then or now.

He wants to put it all behind him? Well, I wish I could easily do that. Will I ever be able to put it behind me? I didn't ask to be placed for adoption. I'm of legal age now. I think I'm entitled to more than an abrupt brush-off from an "adult" who obviously still doesn't want to assume responsibility for his actions.

Sometimes I find myself thinking someone has made a terrible mistake; I really wasn't adopted. Even after meeting Elsa. Those moments pass quickly and reality returns. What do others do and think when they're in my situation?

I wonder if I'm abnormal to question whether others in a situation such as mine think there's been some mistake. Perhaps there are advantages to never knowing you are adopted. I'm uncertain.

After reading all those books about adoption and searching for my birth parents, I'd concluded, especially after meeting Elsa, that adoption was a story of love. Adoptive and birth families share a child by love, rearing, and blood.

I knew love was caring, warmth, strength, and weakness. Love has its own power--that power my birth father held in his hand when he drafted his letter. Birth parents, adoptive parents, and adoptees are bound together in different kinds of love. A birth father, mine, had used love's power and hurt me, whether intended or not.

Adoption **is** about love, but I now know, personally, it's also about pain—the pain of surrendering a child for adoption, the pain of couples who must adopt to have children, and the pain of the child who grows up and lives "adopted," and the pain of being rejected. I was prepared for the love. I wasn't really prepared for the pain or rejection, I guess. I should have been; I had ample warning.

Our lives are much like the game of cards I had so often played when I was a child; I played the cards dealt me. In life, we play the hand life deals us as best we can. There are no other options. Unfortunately, one doesn't always hold the winning cards in a game or in life.

But as Aunt Alex had told me, "This is simply a bump in that long road called life. The road goes on." I had no other choice, just as Dad had no choice. The dark of night always ends with morning. I long for that light. Surely my world will right itself.

When Dad died I lost the only family I'd ever known. Well, there was Aunt Alex and Christine, but that wasn't Mom and Dad. Then I'd discovered I had another family. After discovering one half of my other family, I still had more family out there. I'd longed to find the other half, and I did, only to be rejected.

I'd looked forward to uncovering the final layer of who I am. I know part but long to know all. After Dad died, I thought I was dangling from two strings. I've secured one, but the other has been severed, and by my biological father. I'm hanging over an abyss by one string.

Can I move on?

Epilogue

October 2000

But somehow I did move on. With the support of Alle, Aunt Alex, Christine, Elsa, and The Man above, life improved.

It's been over eight years since Dad's death, twelve since Mom's. I've remained in the house in Malibu. After the weeks of searching for my birth parents, weeks also of wondering if I could stay forever in this house with all the memories, mementoes, and empty rooms, I returned to the University of Arizona for two years of graduate study leading to a Master of Arts in theatre, the degree I needed to teach in a community college.

The house no longer projects loneliness for me. Instead, our two kids fill the once empty rooms with noise and excitement. I now know where I belong; this feels like home once again.

A year after Dad's death and my search, Shelby Alaina Morgan and I married. Yes, in Honolulu, just like Mom and Dad. Alle taught high school English then. She's now a stay-at-home mom to little Erin and Devin. I teach theatre at a nearby community college and see to it that my schedule allows lots of family time.

*****

Over the years Alle and I had seriously dated, we generally had a solid relationship. There had been many "ups" and only one serious "downer."

That downer in our relationship occurred a few years ago.

We'd met as sophomores in September. Our introduction had occurred in the first technical theatre lab class we'd taken. We dated many times during that first semester. Whether accurate, I sensed Alle's interest in me. Following a few more dates, I initiated cooling the relationship and finally didn't ask her for dates. Alle was deeply hurt I was told later, yet still engaged me in conversation when we'd see one another around campus. Looking back on that period, I probably feared eventually being rejected so stopped asking her for dates. In my high school years if I had feared a girl friend's rejection, I ended the relationship. My ending the relationships didn't deeply hurt me, but, no doubt, was hurtful to them. I wish I had been more sensitive to their feelings at the time. This hurtful behavior on my part was unclear to me until after I'd met and talked with my birth mother and had called Alle.

When the situation with the broken light batten and the spilling counter weights occurred, and I heard someone yell, "Everyone, offstage," I had grabbed Alle and taken her into the wings. She asked, "You grab and rush me offstage at that sign of danger, but you have remained aloof for months now. Why is that?"

The question dazed me. "I don't know, Alle. You have to give me time to think about that. It's perplexing when you put it that way."

Giving thought to Alle's question over the course of many days, my brain and emotions finally came into sync. I really liked Alle, had missed her company, and had been foolish. My fear of her rejecting me was hardly rational but present. I made a conscious decision to deal with my fear as best I could and renewed our dating. Doing that was sometimes a struggle, but I usually successfully managed those rejection fears. There were no serious rejection fears which surfaced from the point I clearly understood how much I needed Alle's friendship and closeness. She felt a major part of my wholeness.

Another situation which proved a minor relationship problem occurred early in our senior year. I always avoided telling Alle, and people I met, my father was film star Devin MacArthur. Since I used Bradshaw, Dad's legal surname, concealing my parents' identity was easy until Dad came to campus for a theatre department speech.

Dad and Mom, both having graduated from the University of Arizona Theatre Department, had always contributed handsomely to the Department. Only the Department Chairman and professors knew I was Devin MacArthur's son; students did not. My parents' contributions were always contingent upon my identity remaining unknown to the students unless I divulged the information. The Chairman and faculty had faithfully kept their vow, proving that money talks.

I learned from Dad he would be coming to Tucson to speak to theatre students only about "Careers in Film." Man, I was apprehensive. Alle and I had been dating for almost three years when I asked her to attend Devin MacArthur's speech, but I continued to hide my father's legal name. Of course, she wanted to attend as she had enjoyed Dad's films over the years.

Ending the speech, Dad said, "Few of you know my son is a theatre student here and is in the audience tonight. Since he's a senior, I doubt he will mind my identifying him." Not only did I mind, I wanted to slink away; I felt embarrassed, and I'm sure I turned crimson as another fear surfaced in my brain. Would knowing my father's identity cause Alle to run? Everyone began looking around shortly before Dad said, "Lance, would you please stand?" I was the only theatre student named Lance, so immediately all eyes turned on me.

I reluctantly complied. As I stood, I felt all eyes piercing me. I looked down and saw Alle's flustered expression as she looked up at me.

Dad had a dinner meeting with the chairman and faculty immediately following his speech and had explained earlier that he would meet me back at my house as soon as his dinner concluded.

Alle and I departed the theatre building as soon as Dad's speech ended. None of my peers said anything to me, but I was indeed the recipient of a few admiring and a few surprised expressions.

As we left the building and were out of earshot of others, Alle said her first words, "Lance, why didn't you tell me your father was Devin MacArthur? We've seen some of his movies together, and you knew I liked him on the screen. I'm disappointed and hurt."

"I always knew I should tell you, but feared you would run. My high school girlfriends either were fearful of seeing me again after I identified my father, or they thought I was someone to pursue, a real catch. Both attitudes were scary for me. So I said nothing to you."

"Don't you think failure to tell me was unfair and untruthful?"

"I never thought of it being either, just safe for me. Yeah, I know how selfish that sounds." I paused as a thought raced through my mind. "It was selfish! I'm sorry, but I loved you and certainly didn't want to take any chance of losing you."

Silence reigned for a few seconds. Then Alle said, "You're forgiven, but in the future have more confidence in me."

"I promise."

"Lance, I have to admit had you told me in the beginning of our serious dating, I might have run. Having known you for almost three years, I couldn't do that now. I love you too much."

Still, Alle and Dad didn't meet until the following year when Dad flew out to Tucson to tell me about the cancer returning. I could have arranged a meeting sooner. Why didn't I? Alle had always been a "keeper."

One event, above all others contributed to our becoming closer as a couple. A family medical problem has the potential to heal divisions and bond individuals. The summer between our sophomore and junior years, Alle's father had a serious heart attack. The heart attack came as a shock because there had been no previous indications of heart problems.

The call from Alle had come around midnight.

"Lance, Mom just called. Dad's had a heart attack and is being taken to the Mayo Clinic in Phoenix. I don't want to drive home alone at this hour. Could you take me?"

"Certainly. I'll be at the dorm in a few." I even failed to say how sorry I was. What a dunce?

As soon as Alle had gotten in the car, I said, "I'm so sorry. How is he?"

"I'm not sure. Mom just said it was serious and to get there as soon as I could." The tears flowed.

"Alle, I understand how you must feel having gone through Mom's accident. We can't do much now other than pray. Can't hurt."

Pray we did. While I didn't exceed the speed limit often, I know there were times in the next hour or two when our pieces of conversation and anxiety led me to forget to glance at the speedometer; thus, my foot got a little heavy, I fear.

Locating the hospital and a parking area without difficulty illustrated Alle's capable navigating skills. Thankfully, she'd visited family friends there a few times.

After asking at Emergency Admissions where we could find Jared Morgan, we were directed to the surgical floor. There in Surgery Waiting we found Alle's mom in the waiting room.

"Kris," I said, "we got here as quickly as we could. How is Jared?"

"Lance, he's in by-pass surgery now. The doctor will be out when it's completed."

Alle said nothing, she and her mom just held onto each other.

As we waited, my mind continued to drift back to that time when Dad, Mona, and I had waited for someone to tell us Mom's condition. I felt almost as useless now. Trying to comfort Alle and Kris wasn't easy. What could I really do other than re-plenish coffee? I wanted to hold Alle, but she and Kris provided that comfort each of them needed. I intellectually understood I'd be more comfort to Alle later. Emotionally, I felt I needed to do more than keeping the coffee cups filled, yet I realized on some level my just being present was the comfort I could best offer at the moment.

A thought kept recurring to me over the next two hours or so. How did those with no religious foundation cope with such situations? Who could they call upon for help? I didn't under-stand that.

All three of us prayed. I, and perhaps Alle and Kris, also had fleeting thoughts, had fears, and even had a few pleasant mem-ories. I didn't recall as I sat in the waiting room to hear Mom's condition having any pleasant memories. However, during the time I waited with Alle and Kris those few hours, I often had passing pleasant memories of the times I'd had with Jared when visiting Alle's home.

One memory kept creeping back into my consciousness and was such a happy memory. The first time I'd met Alle's parents had been in their home. Allie had said rather nervously, "Mom and Dad, this is Lance."

Following the usual "Good to meet you" rituals, Jared had said, "Honey, does Lance not have a last name?"

I just boldly blurted, "The last name's Bradshaw. I'm from Malibu, and my parents both graduated from the University of Arizona as did both of you Alle told me."

"Well then, Lance, since you're also progeny of Arizona grads, we'll forgive you for being from Malibu."

I couldn't restrain my laughter and responded, "That's great, and I'll reciprocate and forgive you for being from Scottsdale as my grandmother always lived here."

We both laughed, and our relationship has since been one of mutual respect and admiration.

After what seemed an eternity, the surgeon entered and headed toward us. I stood, but Alle and Kris remained seated. They were exhausted.

The doctor said, "Mrs. Morgan, your husband is now in recovery. The by-pass surgery went well. He will soon be moved to ICU for a few days. He's a strong man, so he will likely recover quickly, and be moved to a regular room."

"Thank you so much, Doctor."

"You're welcome. As soon as he's comfortable in ICU, a nurse will be in, and the three of you will be allowed in the room for a few minutes."

Alle, for some reason, was not prepared to see her father with all those tubes connected to machines. The time for me to provide Alle some physical comfort had come. I moved to place my arm around her. She leaned into me.

All three of us stayed the night, alternating sleeping in the waiting room and sitting in Jared's room. Early the next morning the doctor and nurses removed Jared's breathing tube, and all three of us were allowed to spend a few minutes with him.

He did rally quickly. When Alle was sure that her father would recover soon, we returned to Tucson and our classes.

I've always been amazed how such a serious medical emergency is able to bind a couple closer. Alle and I never looked back. Our relationship grew stronger in the coming months.

Our life is now full and happy.

*****

Christine visits often. She's close to Alle and me and the kids, but also to Aunt Alex. Alex revels in having both a nephew and niece, in addition to having little Erin and Devin around.

Christine's film career has taken flight, her dream now reality. She stays busy, making a social life difficult, but she's often expressed a desire to meet that special someone. Eligible bachelors with whom she comes in contact in the film colony don't interest her for long. Finding someone like Dad in that environment is rare, assuming she's searching for someone like him. Alle and I think that may be what she's looking for. We always attempt to play matchmakers, but to date we've had no success.

Alle and I are active in the church I always attended in Santa Monica. Christine's penthouse is near the church so she attends with us. Little Erin and Devin are being taught the values we and our parents and grandparents thought valuable.

Mona retired a year ago and lives in a condo I bought her in Santa Barbara. We see her often. Ginny, Mona's daughter, now maintains the family working relationship in the household. Ginny and her family continue to live in our guest house. Ginny comes in three days a week to help Alle with the housework and kids. The other staff periodically employed by Dad and Mom are gone. We do have a gardener who maintains the lawn and keeps Mom's rose garden just as she kept it, with some periodic help from me.

When I look at the patio roses in full bloom, I always experience wonderful memories of Mom. I experience similar feelings of Dad when I'm sitting at his desk. Often when I watch little Erin and Devin playing, I'm saddened that they will never know my parents. I'd like to think they are both looking down from Heaven on little Erin and Devin and experiencing great joy watching them but don't think that possible since Heaven is a place of joy. How could Heaven be joyful for those there by looking down on all the pain on earth? I feel blessed the kids have Elsa, Alexa, Christine, and Alle's parents.

My family enjoys walks along the beach where my thoughts always return to the good times Mom, Dad, and I had on the beach and swimming in the ocean. The ocean and the beach are our haven—restful, relaxing, and peaceful.

I often see Billy, Dad's old agent, for coffee, and Alle and I periodically attend his and his wife's parties. We also see Rick and Cliff and their wives socially. Otherwise, I no longer maintain many Hollywood ties, except to continue to help when needed with the charities Dad and Mom always supported. I'm certain Billy still misses Dad, their closeness having grown over the years of their association. I sometimes laugh when Billy gives me the "soft sell" about a film role, but he's now busy representing Christine. How many times do I have to tell him a career in film for me, unlike Dad, never would "float my boat," to use an expression that Aunt Alex often uses? Cliff still performs accounting duties for me, pays the bills, and manages my finances, while Rick continues as my attorney.

Aunt Alexa sold her property in Oklahoma City after Dad died and moved to Santa Barbara. We see her often; Erin and Devin love spending time with their great aunt.

Elsa often flies down from Seattle to spend time with us and her grandkids. Erin and Devin love her dearly. For a number of years, I've been trying to move her to another Santa Barbara condo I bought so she'd be close to us. Someday I think she'll cave and move down. She's a close and dear friend, even though she's my mother by birth. I've grown to deeply love and respect her, but "Mom" and "Mother" are reserved for the one who reared me, changed my diapers, cared for me when I was ill, held me when I was afraid, and loved me each day she was alive. Perhaps there is a day in the future when I can call her "Mom," but I think that moment is sometime in the future. Elsa understands, difficult though it may be for her. She loves me as her son, but accepts my loving her as my birth mother and a very close and dear friend. That's reality. She's not Mom. I bonded with another mother as a baby difficult though that may have been at the outset. It's another of adoption's unavoidable realities. Another reality is that nothing seems missing from my life anymore, and I seldom have fears of rejection. Elsa must have been the missing piece. There's something mysterious about that genetic connection I don't understand as it relates to adoption, but my heart senses its truth.

My college teaching duties and play production schedule keep me busy. During the school year, I accept no other duties, spending as much time as I can with my family and our church activities.

In the summer, when I'm not teaching and directing theatre productions, and time permits, I do some work with the Big Brother organization just as Dad did. Many young people have no positive male influence in their lives as was my fortune.

On October 5th, I came home after my classes, and Alle handed me a note: Ben Cameron called you this morning and asked you to call him back sometime this evening at the number below.

"Did he say what he wanted, Alle?"

"No, just that he needed to talk with you."

"It's a LA number. If you remember, my biological father's name was Cameron. Wonder if we're related? I'll go into the study and call him. Could you hold dinner until I'm finished?"

"Yeah, but if you're too long, I'll just go ahead and feed the kids."

I walked into the study, sat down, and dialed the number. After three rings, I heard "Hello, Cameron residence."

"I'm Lance Bradshaw returning Ben Cameron's call. Is this Ben?"

"Yes, it is. I'm glad you returned my call. We need to talk."

"Okay, I'm listening."

"My father, Hunter Brett Cameron, died a few weeks ago in Bellevue, Washington." I was momentarily stunned. A premonition of the next words from Ben quickly came to my mind. "As Mom and I were going through his desk after the funeral, we found a letter and some pictures to him from a Lance Bradshaw with a Malibu return address."

"I wrote him about eight years ago, shortly after my father died. Dad left me a letter saying he and my mother adopted me through a Seattle agency. Through them, I located my birth mother who said Hunter Brett Cameron was my birth father."

"Mom and I assumed that was the case after we read your letter to Dad. You see, my parents were separated off and on for about a year once. Dad eventually came back home permanently for some reason."

"Then we're half-brothers."

"We are. I live in Los Angeles now. I am a lawyer with Montgomery and Associates in LA."

"You work for Rick Montgomery?"

"Yeah, and he's a great guy. That's how I got your phone number."

"Rick gave it to you?"

"I showed him your letter to Dad and asked for his advice."

"And Rick said?"

"I've known Lance since he was a baby. I'm his attorney as I was his father's. I think Lance would want you to contact him, so…"

"Did Rick tell you anything about me?"

"No, he didn't, and I didn't ask him to do so."

"Are you calling about getting together?"

"Yes. Would you be willing to meet?"

"I think I'd like that."

"When would you want to do this?"

"Whenever it's convenient."

"How about after you get off work tomorrow? Drive out to Malibu and spend the weekend with us."

"I can do that. Give me directions."

After I gave him directions to the house, he said, "Lance, I look forward to meeting you."

"Same here."

"See you tomorrow about five."

The remainder of the evening and all day Friday was spent in anticipation of meeting my brother. Concentrating during my classes proved difficult for me. I couldn't help thinking my birth father didn't want to meet me, but my half-brother did. Ben must be the apple which fell far from the tree.

When I'd asked Ben to come out on Friday, I'd forgotten Christine was spending the weekend with us. I hoped they'd get along. At least Christine was beautiful. Maybe Ben could appreciate that.

The only troubling aspect of meeting Ben was perhaps I'd acted hastily in agreeing to meet. I had no information about him. Why did I invite him for the weekend? That may have been foolish. Why had I not moved slower on all this? While I was eager to finally have this part of my personal puzzle in place, perhaps there was more. Why had I not been more hesitant? There was only one reason, I concluded. Rick! Rick was one of Dad's oldest friends. Dad had always trusted him, and his trust in Rick had always been validated. I also trusted Rick. Ben worked for Rick. Had Rick been at all hesitant about my meeting Ben, he would never have encouraged Ben to call me. Otherwise, he'd have called me himself. I simply had to go with my heart and trust all this would work for the best. This phone call seems like some screenplay, some divine screenplay not a horror one.

Friday afternoon, I heard Ben's call from the security gate shortly after five, pressed the button opening the gate for him, and waited outside near the front door for him to drive up.

When he got out of the car, I noticed he was tall and lean, brown hair, but dark complexioned. Our Italian ancestors! My blond hair, blue eyes, and fair complexion were in stark contrast. He was a handsome guy. The thought crossed my mind that maybe Christine would like this guy. That seemed a really crazy thought at the time.

We shook hands as he said, "Good to meet you, Lance. And thanks for the invitation."

"You're welcome."

The front door flew open and out rushed Erin, aged six, and Devin, four. Devin walked over to Ben, looked up and said, "You my daddy's brother?"

"Yes, I am young man, and I'm also your uncle." Devin looked puzzled and turned to me. I just smiled. "Aren't you a handsome little fellow?" Ben patted his head, messing Devin's hair. Devin withdrew, slightly embarrassed. "And what's your name young lady?"

"Erin," she said sheepishly. "I'm named after my grandmother who's in heaven."

"And I'd bet she'd be proud of you and your little brother."

"Yes," she said beaming. "And I have two other grandmas, too, and a grandpa. And I have two aunts, but they're not red or crawl on the ground." Ben chuckled.

"I'll bet you enjoy playing with all of them, don't you?"

"Yes."

I moved over and touched Erin's shoulder. "Erin, you and Devin go on inside now. Find your mother and Christine and see if dinner is ready. They scampered off.

"Ben," I said, "I'll show you to your room." He got his bag, and we went upstairs. Shortly after coming downstairs, we found Alle and Christine in the kitchen putting the final touches on dinner. "Alle, this is my brother, Ben."

"Glad to meet you, Ben. Welcome to our home."

"Thanks. It's good to meet you also."

I turned to see Christine almost hidden and said, "Christine, this is my brother, Ben." Christine stepped toward him as I said, "Ben, my sister, Christine."

As they shook hands, Ben said, "Delighted to meet you. You look familiar."

"I can't imagine why, Ben," Christine said teasingly.

I looked at Alle. She smiled broadly. I knew why Ben had Christine's attention. He was handsome, seemed down-to-earth, not arrogant unlike many men she encountered. There seemed to be mutual interest though. We'd never seen that before when we'd introduced Christine to eligible men. Interesting, I thought. Of course, I assumed Ben was unmarried for some reason. Was it that I noticed no ring?

"Ben," Alle said, "Christine works in films. Have you ever seen a movie with Christine MacArthur?"

"Of course, I've seen all of them. Forgive me for saying this, but I like looking at you in person, better than on the screen."

"Thank you, Ben. You're kind to say that."

"Oh, I'm dead serious. Meeting you is a pleasure. So you're my brother's sister. Wow."

"Thank you, Ben."

"Ben, there's much more to the story. We are brother and sister, but we aren't genetically related." I could see Ben didn't understand. "It's a long story. We'll explain it over dinner."

Ben turned to me. "Mom and I've wondered about your father. Who was he?"

"Rick didn't tell you his name?"

"No, should he have done so?"

"Not really. Dad was known professionally as Devin MacArthur."

"The actor?" Ben said. "The movie star?"

"Yeah, that's the guy."

"Wow. You're a Hollywood kid."

"No, I'm really not. Mom and Dad moved here before I came along to get away from the Hollywood influence and rat race. They both eschewed much of the Hollywood life. Dad always said, 'Fame is just wind. Sometimes it blows your way. At other times it blows away from you, and then there are those times when the wind is strong enough to destroy you.' Dad and Mom were able to prevent it from destroying them and me. And Christine never lived here. A complicated story best left for later."

"Avoiding publicity was probably not easy for them with all the publicity hounds in a place like Hollywood."

"Probably wasn't, but they did it. I was the beneficiary."

"Okay, guys, dinner is ready," Alle called from the dining room. "Come on to the table."

Over dinner, Ben and I shared as much as we could about our lives, and Christine shared her story. Ben seemed curious about our relationship. I suspected why. We had to talk around all the interruptions from Erin and Devin, but Ben seemed to enjoy the banter. However, I noted the special interest Ben had when we'd shared that Christine and I were not blood related. From that point on, I began to see that Ben and Christine seemed to take much more interest in each other.

After dinner, Ben and I said goodnight to the kids, Alle, and Christine. I kissed and gave each a big hug. Alle and Christine took them upstairs for their baths and a bedtime story. Ben and I went into the study with our refilled glasses of wine.

As we sat, I said, "Ben, tell me about your dad."

"First, Christine's beautiful and interesting. I like her. Hope I can see more of her."

"I think I know a couple who can arrange that. She seemed taken by you."

"She did?"

"Man, you didn't notice?"

"No. Dumb me."

I couldn't help laughing. "Now, tell me about your dad."

"Dad suffered a massive heart attack about a month ago. He was only 59. I'm sure his smoking and terrible eating habits contributed to his fate. He was dead before the ambulance arrived at his office we were told."

"I'm sorry. I'd have liked to have met him. My father had only a few weeks after he found out nothing could be done for his cancer. I'd have liked nothing more than to have had more time with him. My mom was killed in an auto accident shortly after I graduated from high school. Death is painful."

"We always think they're supposed to die in old age, don't we?" He paused before continuing, "Any other family, Lance?"

"My Aunt Alexa, Dad's sister, lives in Santa Barbara. And you know how Christine fits in. My other mother still lives in the Seattle area, but she spends lots of time down here. Alle's parents fly out from Flagstaff periodically also. We're a small family, but we're a happy one."

"I'm an only child also. My mom's well. Still lives in Bellevue, but has been considering selling the house and moving into an apartment so she'd not have home and yard maintenance. I'm encouraging that. We have plenty of aunts, uncles, and cousins around Seattle and Bellevue. You'll have to meet them someday."

"Perhaps, I will. You're not married?"

"Nope, not yet."

"I failed to ask earlier. How's the job going?"

"Great. I like working with Rick. I like living in LA. I prefer the sun and heat here to the clouds, rain, and cool weather in Seattle."

"Yes, Rick's a great guy. I've known him all my life. I know about that Seattle weather having visited there a few times."

"The job here is a real opportunity for me. While I hated to leave Mom in the Northwest, the job was something I couldn't pass up."

"I can appreciate that. Tell me more about your dad."

"Dad was a kind man, but not very inclusive to us at home. He hid his struggles in aloofness, presenting a wall rather than a bridge to cross together. Socially he was an outgoing and friendly guy. He was always well liked but not the most attentive husband or father. He was tall, lean, brown hair and eyes, handsome some would say. You resemble him, Lance, even with different coloring."

"That's what Elsa told me." Ben looked puzzled. "Elsa's my birth mother."

"With whom Dad had the affair?" I nodded, and he continued, "He was employed by an aviation firm and spent vast amounts of time working, whether at home or in his office. Mom always said there was a part of him off-limits to us. That was obviously true."

"Was your mom aware of his affair?"

"We talked about that after we found your letter in his desk and wondered why he kept it. She said they were having problems in 1969 and early 1970, and he left for long periods of time. What my parents' problems were she never explained. Dad would come home for most of a weekend periodically or for an evening, but would always leave again. He refused to discuss it with her. What his problems were, I don't know. Why he came back for good, she was uncertain, but perhaps because she was pregnant with me."

"That must have been really difficult for her. She never suspected an affair?"

"She says she didn't, but she simply may not want to admit it to me."

"Was she hurt, Ben, when you found my letter among your dad's things?"

"She didn't seem to be. If the letter hurt her, she hid that well. She's a very forgiving person, but I suppose she had to be in order to stay with Dad. When I told her I had to locate you, she encouraged. I think she realized it was something I had to do. For me! I really think she approves of my contact. Neither of my parents ever denied me much."

"Ben, did you by any chance bring some pictures? I'd like to see some pictures of him."

"I did. Thought of that at the last minute and threw some in my bag. How about I bring them down when we have breakfast in the morning?"

"That's great. There's one other thing I'd like your reaction to, if you don't mind." He indicated that'd be okay. I got a copy of Ben's father's response to my letter, handed it to him, and waited for him to read it.

After a few minutes, he handed it back and said, "I don't know what to say. His response was cold, a brush-off."

"That was basically my reaction."

"Lance, there's nothing I can say that will make you feel better about it. I know how it must have hurt." After a slight pause, he added, "Maybe he was afraid."

"It did hurt, and perhaps he was afraid. He's no longer with us so any chance of a relationship has passed."

"Neither of us can do anything about it at this point. It's best to let it go. 'To understand is to forgive,' the saying goes. Maybe in this case, to not understand is also to forgive. Anyway, you have me. We're brothers, and we can have a relationship."

"You know, I think I like having a brother. We both grew up without siblings. Now we have them. I'm glad you live in LA."

We both went upstairs a short time later. As I crawled into bed, Alle said, "Lance, I liked him but had been concerned I wouldn't. What did you think of him?"

"Honey, I liked him too, very much. It feels good to have a brother in my life."

"Did you notice Ben and Christine?"

"Yes. Sort of humorous."

"She told me she really liked him."

"Alle, she decided that quickly. She's never made such a decision so quickly before."

"I know, but maybe that's good."

"I know she interests him."

"Lance, I encouraged her to give him her phone number."

"Will she?"

"I think she will before he leaves."

"We'll see." I kissed her goodnight, but sleep didn't come quickly for me. I mentally replayed the evening.

On Saturday, Alle, Ben, Christine, and I had an early swim in the ocean and a late breakfast. Ben brought the pictures down. Looking at them felt surreal. I was looking at a father I never knew I had. Looking at my birth father, I had to agree with Ben and Elsa. There was a resemblance. Later, the four of us drove around Malibu, Hollywood, and LA, places he'd never visited, while Ginny watched the kids.

Sunday, after church, the four of us and the kids came home for lunch, and then it was time for Ben to get back to LA.

Everyone said goodbye in the house except me. I walked with him out to his car, we shook hands, and I said, "Your visit's meant a lot to me. I hope we visit again."

"I'm certain we will, Lance."

Just then Christine came rushing out the door waving a paper. "Ben, wait a minute." She walked over to the car, handed Ben the paper and said, "Here's my address and phone number. Call me."

"Thanks. You bet I will."

As Christine turned to enter the house, I said, "Well, Sis, better late than never."

She looked at me and said, "I may be a late bloomer, little bro, but I do bloom." She winked at me, and said, "Ben, you call me now," as she moved toward the front door. Ben had a big grin on his face.

Ben started the car, but then got out and walked toward me. As he gave me a hug, he said, "I cannot tell you how great it feels to have a brother." He winked and added, "Especially a brother with a sister like Christine."

"Yes, it feels good. Do call Christine. The two of you will get along well."

"Don't worry, Lance. I'll definitely call her." He smiled broadly, turned, and walked to his car.

He got in the car, put it in gear, and headed down the drive toward the gate, but before he was out of my vision, he stuck his arm out the window and waved.

I returned the wave, smiled, and walked to the front door. I felt I had a family again.

Shortly before I fell asleep that evening, I picked up my Bible on the nightstand and reread these verses from Ecclesiastes 3: *For everything there is a season, and a time for every matter under heaven: a time to be born, and a time to die; a time to plant, and a time to pluck up what is planted; a time to kill, and a time to heal; a time to break down, and a time to build up; a time to weep, and a time to laugh; a time to mourn, and a time to dance; a time to cast away stones, and a time to gather stones together; a time to embrace, and a time to refrain from embracing; a time to seek, and a time to lose; a time to keep, and a time to cast away; a time to tear, and a time to sew; a time to keep silence, and a time to speak; a time to love, and a time to hate; a time for war, and a time for peace.*

My time to heal had come. It was not only a time to build, but also a time to embrace and love. I knew there was no longer a bump in the road or a mountain to climb. Morning had come, the morning after all the darkness. My world had righted itself. I felt complete again, whole. I was at peace.

Acknowledgements

My thanks and gratitude to all those who read this manuscript during the revision process. Regardless of whether you read the manuscript once or more than once, your suggestions and comments were always welcomed, appreciated, and proved helpful. However, I alone am responsible for the outcome. I am especially indebted to Sandy, Dina, Vicki Janzen, **Clare Evans**, and Rosemary Macauley.

Some Afterthoughts

The Primal Wound: Understanding the Adopted Child, by Nancy Newton Verrier, mentioned in Chapter 20 was actually published in 1993. I have taken license and advanced the publication date by a year for this story.

As an adoptive parent and a member of the adoption triad (adoptive parent, adoptee, or birth parent), I've had personal experience with many adoption issues. However, this is a work of fiction and not a personal adoption story or the story of anyone I know. I would note though that many in the adoption triad have adoption experiences similar to those in this story. Some individuals embark on searches which span many years, and some have searches which don't end positively. Our search for birth parents lasted well over three long years; many have searches lasting much longer. Regardless of the search length or outcome, I think there is value in searching.

I've had personal experiences which influenced portions of this story but will mention only one of them. When I lived in Fresno, California, about 15 years ago, I had a friend, Glen Janzen, who influenced my life. My memories of Glen are happy ones and continue to provide joy. He was an example worth emulating. During the many months of his terminal illness, he remodeled a house within walking distance of my home. I would walk over a few times a week to see how he was doing and the remodel progress he was making. Each time I'd ask him how he was doing, he'd reply with some variation of, "I read the obituary pages this morning and saw I wasn't listed, so I'm doing fine." That attitude always impressed me and, as you've seen, his statement made its way into this manuscript.